THE RIVERSIDE DANCE STUDIO

NICOLE ELLIS

1

Sam

"Wait up, Mandy," Samantha Briggs called out as she struggled to avoid catching her two-inch heels in the pitted concrete of the dimly lit sidewalk bordering Bayside Prep's campus. When she glanced up to check how far her co-housemother had gotten ahead of her, one heel dug in, and she wobbled precariously before regaining her balance. "Hey, I can't walk that fast!"

"Slowpoke." Mandy offered a toothy grin with her teasing words, but she came to a full stop to allow Sam time to catch up. "You doing okay?"

"Yeah, I'm fine." Sam sighed and ruefully frowned at her silver high heels. They may have been a perfect match for the soft pashmina wrap she wore over a simple black sheath dress, but they certainly weren't comfortable. "I'm rethinking my decision to let my sister talk me into these heels though." Her oldest sister, Libby, had a way of convincing her to buy attire she wouldn't normally choose, claiming it was good for Sam to break out of her comfort zone. Libby may have had a point, but it would all be for naught if the shoes caused Sam to break her ankle before she even arrived at the party. Besides, she'd just gotten back into ballet lessons after many years away from the sport and she didn't want to jeopardize the one thing in her life she was sure about.

Mandy chuckled and pointed to her own spiky shoes, which were a good inch or two taller than Sam's. "Hey, you've got baby heels on compared to mine. Come on, it's a New Year's Eve party. We've got to bring out the big guns. And, by the way, your sister was right—you look amazing in that outfit." Sam narrowed her eyes at Mandy, but her friend just laughed in response. "Don't worry, we're almost there."

Just as Mandy had promised, they rounded a corner, and the rear of the headmaster's home came into view. Sam paused to get a good look at the mansion. "Wow." She'd driven past it before but hadn't gotten the full effect. Now, she had the time to take it all in. The massive red-brick building rose three stories from the ground and was surrounded by a velvety green lawn ringed by towering evergreen trees.

"Impressive, right?" Mandy stopped to appreciate the grandeur as well, falling uncharacteristically silent for a moment. "This campus never fails to fill me with awe."

"No kidding." Sam eyed the white-trimmed dormer windows on the third floor. When she was a kid, her parents had taken her on some historic house tours on the East Coast, but this rivaled anything she'd seen on those trips. "Headmaster Weatherbee actually gets to live here?"

Mandy nodded. "Yup. One of the perks of the job." She cracked a smile. "But hey, who are we to complain?

We get to live in our fabulous dorm rooms and relive our college days."

Sam giggled, relieving some of her pent-up anxiety. "True. I bet the headmaster wishes he could live like us." She glanced at the mansion again. The headmaster's job came with fantastic benefits, but she wasn't sure she'd ever want the stress of being responsible for an entire school.

"I'm sure he and his wife are super envious of us." A huge grin stretched across Mandy's lips as she motioned to the path that continued around to the front of the house. "Are you ready?"

Sam took a deep breath. "I think so." She'd only been teaching at Bayside Prep for two months, and this would be the first real social event she'd attend at the school. While she may seem outgoing and boisterous when teaching a P.E. class, she was an introvert at heart.

In fact, part of her wished that she'd been selected to cover a shift at the dorms that evening to decrease her time at the party. Most of the students hadn't yet returned to school following the holiday break, and a few staff members had been chosen at random for two-hour shifts monitoring the dorms so all of the staff could enjoy at least part of the annual New Year's Eve party.

As they neared the tall white columns framing the front porch, faint notes of classical music drifted through the air as if caught on the light breeze rippling through the sculptured hedges along the circular driveway. The navy-blue door bore a large Christmas wreath made of evergreen boughs, trimmed with a sizable crimson velvet bow.

Sam hung back on the wide porch while Mandy reached for the doorbell, but before her friend had a chance to push the button, the door sprang open, revealing a slender woman in her sixties who beamed at them from the threshold. Her vibrant red lipstick, expertly applied, echoed the hue of her sleeveless satin dress, which boasted a fitted bodice and full skirt that ended mid-calf.

"Mandy! It's been too long. We've got to get together for coffee sometime soon. I want to hear all about your holidays." The woman hugged Mandy, then stood back to admire her electric-blue slip dress. "You look gorgeous. I love how your dress shimmers." She turned her keen eyes to Sam. "And who is this?"

Mandy nudged Sam forward. "This is Samantha Briggs, the new P.E. teacher and housemother in my dorm."

The woman nodded in recognition and smiled warmly at Sam. "Of course! It's nice to finally meet you, Samantha. I've been meaning to get down to the dorms to introduce myself, but things have been so crazy with the holidays." She held out her hand. "I'm Linda Weatherbee, the headmaster's wife. Welcome to Bayside Prep."

Sam reached out to shake Linda's hand, but Linda surprised her by pulling her in for a brief embrace. Sam must have appeared startled, because Linda laughed after she stepped back. "Sorry I couldn't help myself. You looked like you could use a hug."

Sam bit her lip and looked past Linda, into the house. "I'm a tad nervous. I don't know too many people here." As soon as she said that, she winced internally. It wasn't terribly professional to share her concerns with the headmaster's wife, but something about Linda put her at ease.

"Aw, you'll love it here. We don't get a lot of staff or faculty turnover, so I'm sure everyone will be excited to meet you." Linda turned slightly and gestured into the house. "We have appetizers and drinks in the parlor right now, and dinner will be served in the ballroom around seven. Make yourself at home."

A ballroom? Seriously? Sam's apartment in the dorms didn't even have a separate living room. This place was way out of her league. Her stomach clenched, but she managed to eke out a smile and a quick "Thank you."

Linda waved energetically at a couple behind them, which Sam and Mandy took as their cue to enter the house. They followed the music down the hall to a high-ceilinged room that must have been as big as Sam's old apartment. Well-dressed party-goers gathered in clusters in the seating areas and around bar-height tables dotting the room.

"And I thought the outside of the house was impressive," Sam whispered to Mandy.

"I know." Mandy scanned the crowd, her gaze landing on a woman in her late twenties tucked under the arm of a man standing next to her. "There's Annabeth. She teaches high school history. Have you met her yet?"

Sam shook her head. She'd met most of the elementary school teachers already, but not many from the high school. She'd made an effort to get to know the people she worked with, though she couldn't help wondering if it was worth the effort since she was only contracted to work there for a few more months.

"C'mon then." Mandy made a beeline for the woman she'd called Annabeth, and Sam trailed along in her wake. When they reached the couple, the woman gave Mandy a hug.

"Hey, Mandy." Annabeth smiled at them, then focused on Sam. "You must be Samantha, right? I've seen you around campus. I'm Annabeth Murphy and this is my husband, Jasper." She stuck out her hand.

"Call me Sam. Nice to meet you." Sam shook

Annabeth's hand and then her husband's. "Mandy said you teach history?"

Annabeth's face lit up and she nodded vigorously. "I do. I've been teaching at Bayside Prep since the beginning of last year. It's a wonderful school."

"Did you previously teach elsewhere in the area?" Sam asked.

Annabeth rested her hand on her husband's arm. "Actually, Jasper and I are both from Massachusetts, but when his dream job in aeronautics came up in Everton, we decided to try out life on the West Coast."

Sam caught a glimpse of the shadow that momentarily crossed Annabeth's face and gave her a sympathetic smile. "You must miss your family and friends back home."

Annabeth sighed. "I do." She glanced up at her husband, who was a good foot taller than her. He rubbed her arm reassuringly, and Annabeth smiled. "But I think this is good for both of us. We needed a change."

"I can understand that." Sam looked down at the floor. She'd wanted to shake things up in her own life, but she hadn't intended on making quite so many changes all at once. For starters, Brant hadn't just been her long-term boyfriend, he'd been her best friend as well, and she'd thought they could remain friends after she broke up with him. When that hadn't worked out, and then she lost her job at the high school and had to move out of her apartment, it had felt as if her whole world was crumbling out from under her. The temporary position at Bayside Prep had been a lifesaver, offering her both an income and a place to live while she figured out her next move.

Mandy cleared her throat. "I think I'm ready for a drink. Anyone else?"

Jasper looked down at his empty wine glass. "I could use a refill."

The four of them walked over to a bar set up in the corner of the room, serving complimentary wine and beer. After they'd all received their drinks, they moved to the side of the room to continue their conversation. A minute later, a woman Sam recognized as a member of the administrative staff approached their little group.

The woman put her hand on Mandy's shoulder and grinned at the rest of them. "Hey. Do you mind if I borrow Mandy? She was telling me the funniest story yesterday about her trip to Oregon, and some of the others from the office want to hear it too." She motioned to a small cluster of women gathered about twenty feet away.

"Of course." Annabeth narrowed her eyes and pointed her index finger at Mandy. "But if the story is that good, I expect to hear it later too."

Mandy laughed. "I promise." She allowed the newcomer to guide her over to the group of women, leaving Sam alone with Annabeth and Jasper.

Sam stared into her glass of white wine, then took a long sip. She didn't drink alcohol very often, so she intended to limit herself to only two glasses over the course of the night, lest she make a fool of herself in front of so many strangers. Across from her, Jasper shifted on his feet and lifted his glass to his mouth.

Annabeth broke the silence. "Sam, are you from this area?"

Grateful for the softball conversation starter, Sam smiled. "I'm actually from Willa Bay, just south of here. I used to teach at the high school there, but my position fell victim to budget cuts in their P.E. program."

"Oh, I'm so sorry." Annabeth's mouth turned downward. "But I'm glad you're here now."

Sam nodded. "Me too." After a frustrating job search, she was grateful for the position at Bayside Prep, even if it was only for the length of a teacher's maternity leave.

The three of them chatted amiably for about twenty minutes, until Jasper and Annabeth decided to take a short stroll around the grounds before dinner.

That wasn't so bad, Sam thought. She'd actually enjoyed their conversation. *But now what?*

She scanned the room for Mandy and found her friend near the grand piano, deep in conversation with an older man. Sam didn't want to bother her, so she slipped away to the edge of the room and drifted out into the hallway.

The sound of dishes clinking together and the muffled voice of a woman calmly directing the staff floated down the hall. Compared to the main room, though, it was reasonably quiet. Without the commotion of a party and the stress of meeting new people, Sam finally relaxed enough to take in her surroundings.

Tall oil portraits of men lined the wall in front of her, and she soon determined they were past headmasters of the school. She didn't know much about Bayside Prep's history, other than that it had been founded in the early 1900s. She studied one portrait after another, wondering what life must have been like during each of their terms as headmaster, separated by time but connected by the same role at the school.

At one end, appearing intentionally set apart from the others by nearly a foot of blank wall space, hung a painting of a woman. Sam moved closer to inspect the image. Judging by the woman's hairstyle, it had been painted sometime in the 1940s. Who was she?

"That's Lucia Davis," a man said from behind her.

Sam spun around to see Andrew Hodgins, the school's

assistant headmaster. She shot him an apologetic smile. "I'm sorry, I'm not familiar with the name." She gestured to the long row of paintings. "Was she a headmistress here?"

He shook his head. "Not officially. She basically ran the school when her husband left to fight in World War II. That's him." He pointed at a man's image, about halfway down the row. "If not for her, who knows what would have happened to Bayside Prep during the wartime years."

"Huh." Sam peered at the woman, filled with a renewed interest. "She must have lived a fascinating life."

He nodded in agreement. "She must have." He looked lost in thought for a moment. "You know, I think one of our former students compiled a biography about Lucia, even interviewing her extensively while she was alive. Linda Weatherbee manages the school's archives. If you're interested, I bet she can find it for you."

Sam stared at the woman's portrait. Something about the determined glint in Lucia's eyes made her curious to know more about her. "I'd like that. The head of the school seems to have always been a man, so I'd be interested to learn more about her experience."

He gazed at the other portraits and wrinkled his nose. "They look like they're about to go in front of a jury, don't they?"

She laughed. The same thought had occurred to her. "They do look awfully solemn."

He gazed reverently at one of the more recent portraits and gestured at it with a quick flick of his index finger. "That's Franklin Courtley. He was the headmaster when I went here. Great man."

Sam's eyebrows shot up. "You went to Bayside Prep?" Her only interactions with Andrew Hodgins had been when he'd interviewed and hired her, and, later, a brief conversation about the possibility of her pupil, Kimmy, taking ballet lessons. Andrew had been straightforward but reserved in those meetings, and she hadn't been able to read him as a person.

He nodded. "I did. I was one of the locals who received a full scholarship. I don't know where I'd be if it hadn't been for Headmaster Courtley."

He didn't elaborate, and although Sam was curious about what he'd meant, she didn't want to pry. Instead, she asked a safe question. "Did you grow up in Paddle Creek?"

He pressed his lips together into a thin line. "No. I'm from Barsten, a one-stoplight town near the mountains, about thirty miles away." He uttered a sharp laugh. "It didn't have much to offer."

"Oh." She wasn't sure what to say, but pressed on to avoid an awkward silence. "Do you still have family there?"

He nodded curtly. "I do. My parents still live in the house I grew up in, along with my sister and her daughter." He shoved hands in his pockets and looked at her indirectly. "You used to teach in Willa Bay, right? Did you grow up there?"

"Yes. I was born and raised in Willa Bay. I didn't even go far for college." Happy memories flashed through her mind—playing with her sisters on the beach while her parents watched from their plaid picnic blanket nearby, baking in the kitchen with her mom, and more recent visions of parties at the Inn at Willa Bay with both family and friends. She swallowed hard, fighting a sudden wave of homesickness.

He nodded in understanding. "It seems like you miss it."

"I do." Her words echoed Annabeth's from earlier, but

Sam hadn't moved all the way across the country—only forty-five minutes from her hometown. She forced a smile. "I'm not that far away, so I can still go home for weekly family dinners and other things." It still seemed like she was missing out on a lot at home though, and the temporary nature of her position didn't help her feel any less adrift. But she couldn't change any of that now. Instead, she reflected on everything she'd seen that evening—the faculty and their guests gathered in the room down the hall, and the house so tastefully decorated, perfectly complementing the natural beauty of the school's setting. "I really do like working at Bayside Prep and living on the campus. It's beautiful here."

"It is." He adjusted his wire-rimmed glasses and viewed the portraits with a wistful expression. "I hope to stay here for a long time."

Sam had just worked up the nerve to ask him to elaborate, when a few people came out of the parlor, chatting as they walked toward the ballroom. She and Andrew stepped to the side as their co-workers filed out into the hall and swept past them.

"Dinner must be ready." Andrew touched her arm lightly, startling her with the sudden personal contact. "The ballroom is this way." He then turned on his heels and strode away, pausing only once to make sure she had followed.

So much for that. Their brief connection had broken, and she doubted she'd ever see him let his guard down again.

In the ballroom, Andrew made his way to the front with single-minded focus. Sam stood at the back, both to get her bearings and to fight off the sense of overwhelm.

She'd almost made up her mind to take a seat at the

nearest table, when a sea of sparkling blue fabric filled her peripheral vision. Relief flooded over Sam.

"Hey! There you are. I've been looking for you." Mandy's cheeks were flushed as she squeezed Sam's arm. She was clearly in her element here. "Isn't this party amazing? I swear, it gets better every year."

"Uh-huh. I've had a good time meeting people." That much was true. While she hadn't been a social butterfly like Mandy, she'd had some good interactions with Annabeth and Jasper, as well as a surprisingly nice time with Andrew.

"I heard you were talking with Andrew in the hallway earlier." Mandy wiggled her eyebrows. "He's pretty cute, isn't he?"

Cute? Sam glanced across the room at Andrew. After breaking up with Brant, she'd sworn off dating for a while and hadn't allowed herself to think about men in that way.

She supposed Andrew *was* attractive, with medium brown hair and kind eyes, but he wasn't the type of guy women usually swooned over.

"I guess so?" Sam answered.

Mandy sighed dramatically. "You guess so? He's smart, handsome, and just a nice guy, overall." She scrunched up her face. "Maybe a little too nice for me, but I could see him as your type."

Sam wasn't sure if she should appreciate that Mandy was thinking about her or be offended that she'd automatically assumed Sam was looking for a nice guy. Brant had been a nice guy too, but after many years with him, she'd had to admit they lacked a certain mutual chemistry. Besides, she had enough uncertainty in her life right now and didn't need to add the complexities of a romantic relationship to the mix.

Sam smiled placidly at her friend. "We had a pleasant

conversation, but that's it. I'm not looking to date anyone right now."

Mandy shrugged. "Okay, suit yourself."

The tables were filling up, and Mandy grabbed her hand. "Let's sit with Annabeth and Jasper."

Sam let her friend pull her over to the table with the couple they'd talked to earlier. Another couple soon joined them, and introductions were made.

At the front of the room, Headmaster Weatherbee approached the microphone stand. He tapped it a few times. "Is this thing on?" He grinned at his guests in a more casual manner than Sam had previously seen him exhibit. Everyone laughed, then quieted so he could continue. "I hope everyone's had a good time so far tonight. I know Linda and I have enjoyed opening our home to all of you." A smattering of applause rippled through the room, and he beamed at them. "And there's more to come. After dinner, we'll clear away the tables and have music and dancing, followed by a Champagne toast at midnight." He went on to thank everyone for making Bayside Prep an amazing place to live, learn, and work. Linda soon joined him, and he wrapped an arm around his wife's waist, pulling her close. "Now, let's eat, then get this party started." He pumped his fist in the air, and Sam fought to hold back a snort of laughter at the unexpected gesture.

Everyone clapped, then returned to conversing with their tablemates while waiting for a staff member to come around to let them know when it was their turn for the buffet. Though it wasn't quite as good as the food from her mom's catering business, Sam thoroughly enjoyed the beef medallions in mushroom sauce, roasted fingerling potatoes, and vegetable medley.

With the help of wine, good food, and friendly tablemates, she became immersed in lively conversation and even managed to get out on the dance floor for a few songs. By the time the clock struck midnight and they'd all wished each other a happy New Year, her feet ached and her heart was full—so full that she wondered if she was letting herself get too attached to a place she'd have to leave in a matter of months.

2

Andrew

Andrew pulled his Toyota Corolla onto the main highway and set the cruise control to fifty miles per hour. He'd driven this road more times than he could count. Admittedly, he hadn't gone home very often lately, much to his mother's dismay, but he'd resolved to do better in the new year. He'd been home only a week ago to celebrate Christmas with his family, and he'd promised her then that he would be back for lunch on New Year's Day because he'd have the day off.

Andrew had grown up in the sleepy town of Barsten, Washington, counting the days until he could leave home. When he'd been awarded a scholarship to a small private college in California, he'd jumped on the opportunity. After graduation, his mother had been ecstatic about his job offer at Bayside Prep. He knew she'd been hopeful that living only an hour away would encourage more frequent visits home.

That hadn't happened though. His chest constricted

and he wrapped his fingers around the steering wheel so hard that his knuckles whitened. Thinking about where he'd grown up always made him a little anxious. He inhaled deeply and forced himself to look at the scenery. The road to Barsten followed the winding curves of the Nahquiat River as it approached the foothills of the Cascade Mountain Range. Even in the middle of winter, the Linden County countryside never failed to awe him with its beauty.

On one side of the road, family farms sprawled in neat squares of acreage, each of them similar to the one he'd been raised on. On the other side, pockets of houses stood sentry over the river. Some were built on stilts, while others took advantage of natural higher elevations to withstand all but the worst of flooding when the spring snow melts turned the lazy river into a rushing torrent. In the summer, his sister, Liv, used to love picking the wildflowers in the grassy areas adjacent to the road's shoulder. The happy memory helped to ease the tension in his shoulders and he lightened his grip on the steering wheel.

The miles flew by, and soon he was turning onto the dirt road leading to his parents' farm. At the moment, the dusty brown fields lay dormant, but in the spring, they'd come to life once again. The fertile grounds were a source of pride and joy for his father, a third-generation farmer on the two-hundred-acre farm.

Trees formed a yard around the two-story farmhouse and provided both year-round privacy and shade during the summer. The exterior had been kept up through the years, although the white paint had cracked in places and muddy boot prints stained the wide porch steps. Andrew parked in front of the house, next to an aging Ford sedan and a newer Kia SUV. Both his mom and sister were home, but his father's work truck was noticeably absent. Good.

He knocked on the door, but no one answered, so he turned the knob and let himself in. Most people locked their doors in Paddle Creek, but here in Barsten, doors were left unlocked more often than not.

"Hello?" he called out as he stepped inside and removed his loafers. His mother had long ago instituted a "no shoes in the house" policy in an attempt to keep the fields outdoors, where they belonged. "Mom? Liv?"

Still no answer, but the house smelled like a bakery, so he assumed someone was home. He walked down the hall and found his ten-year-old niece, Kinsey, sitting on the couch, her knees drawn to her chest to prop up a clipboard. A pair of headphones that he recognized as a Christmas gift hugged her ears, and she tapped a pencil against a piece of paper attached to the clipboard, deeply engrossed in whatever she was doing.

Andrew grinned. Kinsey was big on jump scares, and he'd just been given the perfect opportunity to sneak up on her. He tiptoed toward her and then said loudly, "Kinsey!"

Her gaze shot up and her pencil traced an errant line across the paper as she dropped the clipboard. "Uncle Andrew! That was mean!" She picked the clipboard back up and furiously erased the pencil marks. "Now I can't read my math homework."

He instantly regretted sneaking up on her. "Sorry, Kins. Is there anything I can do to help?"

She sighed loudly in a preteen fashion that signaled the end of the world must be near. "No. I'll fix it." She nodded her head in the direction of the hallway. "Mom's in the kitchen. She came home from work to make sure I was actually doing my math homework." She pouted. "I can't believe stinky Mrs. Anderson assigned homework over winter break anyway."

He tried to hide a smile. He remembered feeling the same way about teachers who'd done that to him when he was in elementary school. "Well, then, I guess I'll leave you to it."

"Make sure to tell Mom that you saw me working on it," she called out. "And ask if she'll bring me some of those cookies she's baking."

Andrew nodded. As he continued down the hall, the aroma of freshly baked chocolate chip cookies grew stronger.

Liv had her back to the kitchen door while she took a tray out of the oven and set it on the stove. "There's already some cooling on the table," she said without turning around.

"Don't mind if I do." Andrew plucked one from a wire rack and bit into it, letting the bits of chocolate melt against his tongue. Liv was famous for her cookies, and it almost made the visit home worthwhile—almost.

She whirled around and narrowed her eyes at him. "I thought you were Kinsey. I didn't know you were coming over today."

He shrugged. "I promised Mom that I would." He finished the cookie and grabbed another before she could swipe his hand away.

She shook her finger at him. "No more. I'm making these for the bake sale at Kinsey's school." She glanced at the vintage black and white clock ticking away on the wall above the kitchen table. "Shoot. I've got to get going. I promised Dad I'd be back soon to go over the spring planting schedule." She frowned. "I hope Kinsey's working on her math. She swore to me she didn't have any homework and then suddenly remembered it the day before she had to go back to school."

"She was hard at work when I saw her in the living room. I'll make sure she finishes it, okay?" He reached for another cookie, but this time, she successfully slapped his hand away while glaring at him.

"You've already had two." Her stern expression faded. "But thanks for offering to help with Kinsey. I feel bad that I've had to work so many hours over her winter break."

The anguish on her face made him swallow hard. When Liv had found out she was pregnant during her sophomore year of college, she'd had to drop out and move back home. Their parents were just making ends meet with the farm and never had much money to spare, and they'd done their best to assist Liv by giving her a place to live and helping her with Kinsey, but it hadn't been easy for any of them. At the time, Andrew had been working at a high school in California and hadn't been able to help much either.

With Kinsey's dad out of the picture, Liv had grown up fast. She started by working full-time for the family business, then went back to college and earned degrees in both agriculture and business when Kinsey was a bit older. Although Andrew would never admit it to her, he considered his sister to be Super Mom and was a little awed by her.

He flashed her a grin. "I'm sure Kinsey had the time of her life, playing video games and lazing on the couch for two weeks. Besides, Mom was here too. I don't think you have anything to feel bad about."

Her lips quivered. "Still... I wish I'd had more time to spend with her. I'm hoping my plans for the new crops pan out and I'll be able to afford to take her somewhere next year."

"Hey." He met her gaze. "Seriously. Don't stress about it. There are several kids at my school who didn't even get to see their families for the holidays. You've done a great job with Kinsey, and she knows you're always there for her."

Liv swiped at her eyes with the back of her hand and managed to eke out a small smile. "Thanks."

"Of course. That's what big brothers are for." He reached for the cookies again, but stopped when he saw her expression. "I had to try."

She sighed loudly, reminding him of her daughter. "These cookies need to cool, but I have to go. Promise you won't eat any more?"

He held up his two fingers, one of the only things he still remembered from his Cub Scout pack. "Scouts honor."

She laughed. "I know what you were like as a Scout, and I'm not reassured." She reached for the winter jacket she'd hung over one of the kitchen chairs and slid her arms into it. "Mom's in her craft room, but she should be almost done by now."

Done? He started to ask Liv what she meant, but she was already down the hall talking to Kinsey. He eyed the cookies, but remembered the promise he'd made to his sister and reluctantly forced himself away from the table.

In the hall, he headed in the opposite direction of the living room, passing the staircase to the upper floor. He paused in front of his mother's craft room, eyeing the slightly open door. He knocked, then pushed on it. Tammy Hodgins faced away from the entrance, walking rapidly on a treadmill while watching a TV show on an iPad she'd placed in the treadmill's device holder.

He approached her, and she tapped the screen to pause the show. "I'll be done in a few minutes. I think Liv made cookies if you want one."

"I had a couple already." He lifted an eyebrow as he examined the exercise equipment. "I was wondering where you were going to put this." His dad had given her the treadmill for Christmas, and Andrew had thought it an odd gift. Although Tammy had always been physically active as the wife of a farmer, she had slowed down in recent years and gained a few extra pounds when her knees started giving her trouble. Since she had never said anything about wanting to exercise indoors, Andrew had secretly wondered if his father had given her the treadmill as a passive-aggressive response to the weight gain.

The machine beeped and she turned it off. "Whew." She wiped the sweat off her brow with a white washcloth hanging over the side of the treadmill. "I'm really out of shape."

Anger at his father flared through him. "No, you're not."

She laughed. "Thanks, honey, but I know I'm not as fit as I used to be. When your dad got me this for Christmas, I wasn't sure about it, but it's exactly what I needed. I'd mentioned to him that I missed walking around the farm, but it was just too cold for me in the winter." She smiled and hopped down from the treadmill. "I couldn't believe he actually thought of it on his own—he's not exactly known for his gift-giving skills."

"Nope. He sure isn't. Remember the subscription to Time Magazine that he gave you for your birthday one year?" Andrew vividly remembered her look of surprise when she'd opened the white envelope with the gift certificate inside. She'd recovered quickly and thanked his dad profusely, but Andrew and Liv had laughed about her reaction for years afterward.

"Oh, believe me—I remember." She chuckled, then dropped the washcloth into a small laundry hamper. She paused in the doorway and turned back to him. "Are you ready for lunch? I made some of my famous egg salad for sandwiches."

"Sounds good." He followed her down the hall to the kitchen, where she quickly retrieved lunch items from various storage spaces around the room. "Do you need any help?"

"Nope." She was rummaging around in the refrigerator, her voice muffled by the door. "Here we go." She shut the refrigerator and carried a red-lidded Rubbermaid container over to the table, along with a loaf of wheat bread and a bowl of clean Romaine lettuce leaves. She set them down, then grabbed a bag of potato chips from a cupboard, along with two plates and a serving spoon.

Andrew put two pieces of bread on each of their plates and opened the plastic containers while she fetched two glasses of water. "Looks good, Mom. This has always been one of my favorites."

"You know, if you came home more often, I would make it for you." She grinned at him sweetly.

He sighed. "I'll try. I'm just so busy with work."

She patted his hand, then spooned egg salad onto her bread. "I know, honey, I was just kidding. You and Liv are both so dedicated to your jobs. I live in the same house as Liv, and it still feels like I barely see her." She arranged a leaf of lettuce on the bread and brought the sandwich to her mouth.

"Well, I bet that makes Dad happy," he muttered under his breath. "At least he got one kid who's as obsessed with the farm as him." He popped a potato chip into his mouth and crunched into it.

Tammy raised an eyebrow and set her sandwich back down on the plate. "What's that supposed to mean?"

His heart raced. He'd intended to keep this visit peaceful and to not let old wounds interfere with his relationship with his mother. In an even tone, he said, "Just that Dad stopped caring about me as soon as I moved to Paddle Creek to finish high school at Bayside Prep. I think it made him realize I was serious about not joining him in the farm business. He never forgave me for that." His eyes burned and he focused on his food to keep his mind off how hurt he'd been by his dad's sudden abandonment.

She peered at him, her eyes full of compassion. "Of course he would have loved for you to eventually take over the farm, but he never expected it from you—or from your sister. He knew you wanted something different for your life."

"Then why did he stop coming to my games when I played for Bayside Prep?" His dad had taught him how to play baseball at a young age and had bragged to everyone he knew about his son being the only sophomore on the varsity baseball team at the local high school. However, when Andrew had left for Bayside Prep, his father hadn't even attended one game. At first, Andrew had thought it was because most of the games were further away, but even when they'd played a school near his hometown, his father hadn't bothered to go.

His mother blinked a few times, then opened her mouth to speak, but was interrupted by his niece entering the room. "Okay, I'm hungry now," Kinsey announced.

Tammy motioned to the food on the table. "Help yourself."

Kinsey piled a plate with a sandwich and a mound of

potato chips. She pulled out a chair, but didn't sit, her gaze bouncing between the two of them, as though she'd just noticed the tension vibrating across the table. "Uh, is it okay if I take this back to the living room to eat? I still have some homework left to do."

"Sure." Tammy got up and tore a paper towel off of the roll hanging from the wall near the sink. "Take this in case you spill."

Kinsey pouted, but took it from her. "I'm not going to spill, Grandma. I'm not a baby anymore."

"Uh-huh. Tell that to the spot on the living room carpet from the orange juice you dropped on the floor last week." She eyed Kinsey pointedly.

Kinsey's face reddened. "That was an accident. The cat startled me."

Tammy smiled at Kinsey. "Still. Take it with you, just in case."

"Fine." Kinsey stomped off with her plate and the paper towel.

"Well, she's going to be fun as a teenager," Andrew remarked.

"No kidding. I'm always telling Liv that this is payback for how she acted as a preteen." His mom sat back down at the table and ate a bite of her sandwich. When she finished chewing, she focused her attention on him. "We were talking about you and your dad, weren't we?"

He gritted his teeth. "I think we were done." He'd already said too much, and talking about it wasn't going to change the past.

She cocked her head to the side and regarded him for a moment, then reached for the bag of chips and transferred a handful of them to her plate. "You know, honey, at some point you're going to have to realize that your father isn't the ogre you make him out to be."

Andrew gave her a tight-lipped smile, fervently wishing that Kinsey had joined them for lunch. He glanced at the open doorway, hoping for a miracle, but his niece didn't materialize.

His mom shook her head sadly. "We don't have to talk about it anymore if you don't want to." She sipped from the glass of water in front of her, then looked up at him. "How are things going at work? I don't think you said much about it at Christmas."

He smiled, tension easing. Unlike his relationship with his father, his work at Bayside Prep brought him joy and was always something he was happy to talk about.

3

_____

Libby

"Do you have enough socks and underwear?" Libby asked Gabe as she watched him pack. She sat on their bed with her back against the headboard, her knees drawn up to her chest. For weeks, she'd been hoping and praying that Gabe would miraculously find a job in the area and not have to move to Idaho, but it was looking like she was going to have to accept it.

Gabe uttered a light sigh, although he didn't roll his eyes like he usually did when she worried excessively. "Yes, honey, I think I have enough to get me through the next ten years. You must have bought out the whole department store."

She pressed her lips together to keep from bursting into tears. She'd gone shopping for everything she could think of that Gabe might need during their time apart. "I didn't want you to run out."

He set the pile of old shirts he'd been holding into a

box labeled "Goodwill" and gave her a gentle smile. "They have stores in Boise, you know."

"I know," she whispered. He probably hadn't needed any of it, but this was one last thing she could do to show how much she cared for him. They'd recently gotten back to a good place after a rough patch in their marriage, and then Gabe's new employer had him transferred to their office in Idaho.

Gabe pushed on the empty bottom drawer on his side of the dresser. The drawer slid smoothly along its rails, shutting with a finality that made Libby wince. She glanced at the open closet. Everything on her husband's side was gone.

He noticed her gaze and tried to lighten the mood. "Hey, just think—you've always wanted more closet space."

That did it. The tears she'd fought to hold back streamed unabated down her freshly scrubbed cheeks. He crossed the room and handed her the box of tissues she kept on her nightstand. She grabbed a handful and mopped at her face, but she couldn't stop crying.

Gabe slid onto the bed next to her and wrapped his arms around her. "I'm sorry, honey."

"It's not your fault. I know you had to take the transfer. It's just so hard." Libby sniffled into what must have been her forty-sixth Kleenex of the night, then buried her head against his chest. "What are the kids and I going to do without you?"

He squeezed her close. "You'll all be fine. You're stronger than you think."

She swallowed hard, but it did little to alleviate the lump that had built up in her throat. She reached for another tissue. This wasn't how she'd envisioned her last night at home with Gabe. As if on cue, a little girl's cries rang out from down the hall, and Libby started to get up.

Gabe released her and put a reassuring hand on her shoulder. "I've got this. Why don't you go splash some water on your face. That always seems to make you feel better."

She nodded, taking a stabilizing breath as she watched him walk out of the room. How was she going to handle being a single parent until the end of the school year? While she realized that many people successfully solo-parented their children, it didn't make the task any less intimidating. She counted on Gabe for a lot, and with four kids under the age of twelve, the next five months would be a challenge.

By the time she finished freshening up in the bathroom, Gabe was waiting for her in bed. He'd left his lamp on and was reviewing something on his phone, most likely his packing checklist. He took his glasses off and smiled at her. "Kaya had a bad dream. I gave her some water and tucked her back in bed with Little Bunny. I started to tell her a quick bedtime story, but she fell back asleep before I even made it halfway through." He searched Libby's face. "You look like you're feeling better."

She slid between the clean flannel sheets and snuggled up against him, resting her hand on his chest. "I am."

"Good." He turned off the bedside lamp and reached for her, his lips meeting hers in the dark. "Because I don't want to waste our last night together."

"I don't either." Libby focused on her husband being there, right next to her in their bed. He'd leave tomorrow —but for tonight, she could pretend that everything was fine.

~

"William, do you want any scrambled eggs?" Gabe stood behind their eldest son, holding a spatula and frying pan.

William nodded, not even slowing down as he chomped his way through a third piece of toast. Gabe shook his head as he doled out a mound of eggs on his son's plate and smiled conspiratorially at Libby, who was seated across the table. "This kid is going to eat us out of house and home. I bet he'll have grown another foot by the time you guys move out to Boise this summer."

Libby smiled back at him as though everything was fine, but in reality, she was a mess. For the sake of their kids, she was trying to pretend it was just another ordinary day, even when everyone knew it wasn't. Their dad was leaving, and they wouldn't see him again for over a month. During the winter, the mountain passes between Western Washington and the interstate highway to Idaho could be treacherous, and flights across the state weren't cheap. They'd budgeted for Gabe to come home to Willa Bay every other month, and she planned to visit him with the kids while they were on spring break.

Libby took a deep breath to remind herself to slow down and enjoy the moment, something she wasn't great at doing. Her exaggerated movement caught the attention of her eldest daughter.

"Are you okay, Mom?" Beth asked.

Libby nodded and got up from the table, clearing away her own plate and Kaya's. "I'm fine. Just thinking about what I need to get done today."

Beth eyed her as though she didn't quite believe Libby's explanation, but she didn't press the issue.

Gabe glanced at the clock. "Time to leave for school."

The kids grumbled, but they dutifully rinsed off their dishes and set them in the dishwasher. The older children grabbed their backpacks and jackets from their assigned cubbies in the entry hall and lined up at the door in front of Gabe. One by one, he gave them big hugs and they said their goodbyes.

Libby busied herself with organizing coats in their hall closet while she kept out of Gabe's way. She wanted him to have this time with the kids, because he planned to leave right after they left for school. Soon, only Kaya remained, and Libby sent her to play in her room while Gabe finished packing.

Gabe carried the remainder of his belongings out to his car. By now, Libby had given up all pretenses of cleaning, and was watching him silently from her perch on the stairs.

He came back into the house, closed the door, then looked at her, his hands shoved securely into his coat pockets.

She bit her lip and looked up at him. "Are you leaving now?"

He sighed. "I need to get going if I want to be there before dark."

She stood, calling up the stairs to Kaya. "Come say goodbye to Daddy."

Kaya bounded down the stairs and hurled her little body against her father, wrapping her arms around his waist. "Promise you'll call me?" Her lower lip quivered.

He hugged her close and kissed the top of her head. "I promise. And I'll be thinking of you kids and Mommy every day. I can't wait until we can all be together again."

"Me too." Kaya sniffled and clung to him more tightly.

"Hey." He gently peeled her away from his legs and crouched down to her level. "I hear there's a really cool amusement park near where I'll be living. Do you think you'd like to go there when you come to see me?"

She perked right up. "Really? Like with a real-life roller coaster?"

He nodded solemnly. "Yep. Lots of roller coasters and an ice cream parlor with the biggest scoops of ice cream you've ever seen."

Her eyes were as huge as saucers. "Whoa. Little Bunny is going to be so excited! I need to go tell her." She gave him a quick hug. "Love you, Daddy."

As Kaya ran back up the stairs to her room, Libby moved closer to Gabe. "Well, that seemed to have taken her mind off of you leaving."

He searched her face. "If only the promise of roller coasters and ice cream worked as well on you."

She laughed, trying to memorize every bit of their last moments together for the next few weeks. "You didn't say anything about the ice cream parlor having mocha-almond-fudge ice cream. If you had, that might have done the trick."

He circled his arms around her waist, and she melted against him. They stood with her head pressed into the crook of his neck and his head resting gently against hers. After a few minutes, Libby reluctantly untangled herself from his embrace and stepped back.

"You should get going." She wiped away a tear with the back of her hand, grateful she hadn't bothered to put on any makeup yet. She'd known it would be a tough morning, and while she usually tried to get herself ready before the kids woke up, there was no point in applying mascara that would be washed away by nine AM.

"I know." He sighed and ran his fingers through his hair. His eyes were slightly red, and while she hadn't seen him crying, she wondered if he'd done so in secret. He reached for her again and gave her a long, deep kiss that made her legs wobble. "But I don't want to go."

She managed a faint smile and gently pushed him away. "You don't really have a choice." She forced a brighter voice. "But as you keep reminding me, we'll see you in a little over a month. It'll go by faster than we expect."

He sighed again and lines of misery were etched into his face. "I hope so."

"I'm going to get you a cup of coffee for the road." Libby swept out of the entry hall and into the kitchen, hoping a change of scenery would help her to gather herself. She filled a large Yeti mug with freshly brewed coffee and grabbed a wrapped biscotti from the plastic bin on the counter.

When she returned, Gabe had already put on his jacket and was placing his wallet in the back pocket of his worn blue jeans. He moved closer to the front door, but only opened it part way, as if he didn't want to fully commit to leaving.

Libby walked over to him and handed him the coffee and biscotti. "A little something for the trip."

"Thanks, honey." With his hands full, he gave her a quick peck on the lips, then hurried out the door. He didn't look back at her until he'd reached his car and leaned inside to set the cup in the center console. Then, he stood fully and gave her a wave.

She smiled and blew him a kiss. He made a production of catching the imaginary kiss and holding it close to him, an inside joke they'd started when they were dating.

"Love you," Gabe called out before getting into his car.

"Love you too." Libby watched as he shut the car door, carefully backed the vehicle out of their driveway, then drove down the street.

When he was out of sight, she closed the door and

collapsed on the couch, allowing herself a few minutes to cry before picking herself up to get ready for the day.

After taking a shower and getting dressed, Libby dropped Kaya off at preschool. Then, she drove to the Sea Star Bakery, located on Main Street in downtown Willa Bay.

Earlier in the week, she'd made plans to meet her good friend Zoe for coffee at their friend Cassie's bakery. Libby had known that Gabe's departure would hit her hard, and she'd need something to cushion the blow. Some people might schedule a manicure or massage to take their minds off of their troubles, but Libby wanted nothing more than to hang out with some good friends.

Although the bakery was likely slammed earlier in the day, by ten o'clock it wasn't too busy. Libby found a parking spot nearby and joined Zoe at a table in the corner of the small eating space.

"Hey, you." Zoe stood when she noticed Libby. She gave her a big hug, then stepped back. "What do you want to order? It's on me."

"Oh, you don't have to do that. I'm just glad you were able to meet me here this morning." Libby may have declined Zoe's offer, but her friend's generosity with both her time and money meant a lot.

"Of course." Zoe gave her another quick hug. "I know this must be tough for you."

"It is." Libby looked down at her hands, twisting her wedding ring. She blinked and looked back up at Zoe. "But it'll be okay. We'll get through this."

"And some yummy food will help." Cassie appeared from behind Libby. Her cheeks were flushed, and strands of wavy blonde hair had escaped the tight bun she'd fixed at the nape of her neck. "Pastries make everything better."

Libby grinned as she eyed the tray of baked goods that

Cassie set on the table. "Exactly how many people were you expecting to cheer up?"

Cassie laughed and re-wound her hair into a bun. "Oh, just a small army. But after the morning I've had, you're going to need to fight me for them."

"What happened?" Libby asked as she reached for a cherry Danish. She bit into it and rich, creamy cheese laced with a generous dollop of cherry pie filling oozed out.

Cassie sighed, pulled out a chair, and plopped down in it. "On top of the normal morning crowd, we had a big order for Teacher Appreciation Day at the elementary school."

Libby wrinkled her nose. "Shoot! I forgot to send something for the kids' teachers. I'd meant to make those salted caramel brownies everyone likes so much." She'd always taken pride in being on top of everything with the kids, but apparently Gabe's departure had already taken a toll on her organization skills.

"I'm sure they'll be happy to get something from you on a different day." Zoe patted Libby's arm. "Spread out the appreciation and all."

Libby grinned. Zoe always knew what to say to make her feel better. "Thanks. That's a good idea."

They'd been chatting about trivial topics for about half an hour when Zoe asked, "Did you hear that Shawn's sister, Jessa, is going to be in town in a couple of weeks?"

"Really?" Cassie asked. "I thought she was in Germany or something."

Zoe shrugged, then reached for the platter of treats. "She is, but she had some leave to use up and Shawn hasn't seen her in a few years. It'll be the first time Celia gets to meet her too." She set the snickerdoodle she'd chosen on her plate and took a sip of coffee. "I have to

34

admit, I'm curious to see what she's like. Shawn talks about her often, but we've been together for almost a year, and it feels weird to not have met her yet. He's visited with my brother and grandfather several times already."

"How long is she going to be here before she has to go back?" Libby leaned forward and selected a small pecan tart from the rapidly dwindling supply of baked goods in front of them. Normally, she'd limit herself to one goody with her coffee, but today she deserved to treat herself.

"I don't know." Zoe scrunched up her face. "She was a little vague with Shawn and he didn't try to pin her down." She sighed. "I wish I knew though. She's staying with Shawn, but I'm going to feel guilty if she decides to stay longer and we haven't prepared one of the cottages for her. After all, she's as much of an owner of the resort as Shawn or the rest of us."

"That is tricky." Cassie cast a glance at the line in front of the curved glass bakery case and grimaced. "I'd better get back to work. It looks like my assistant is getting slammed with the coffee break crowd."

Zoe checked her watch. "I should get back to the Inn too. I promised Tia I'd go through this week's event bookings with her."

They all rose from their seats and Cassie swiftly cleared their table to the nearby bussing station.

"Thanks for the yummy pastries." Libby threaded her hands through the sleeves of her teal puffer jacket and pulled the zipper up. It may have been warm in the bakery, but outside would be a different story.

"You're welcome." Cassie hugged each of them but didn't linger. She called over her shoulder as she made her way back to the counter, "Are we on for next Tuesday morning? Maybe Meg and Tia will be able to make it next week."

"Works for me." Zoe fastened the last button on her gray wool peacoat.

"Me too." With Gabe gone, Libby was happy to have something to look forward to.

She and Zoe left together but split up on the sidewalk to go their separate ways. Libby had paperwork waiting for her on her desk at home for the catering business she owned with her mother, but she couldn't face going back to an empty house quite yet. She got in her car and drove to the supermarket to pick up a few extra things for the kids' lunches and then ran some other errands—anything to keep her mind off of Gabe's absence.

4

Sam

Sam traced her pen down the side of the notebook page as she assessed her January lesson plans for the elementary grades. The kids had learned about individual sports for most of the first semester, but they'd soon switch over to building skills in team sports. She was tapping the end of the pen against her lips, deliberating between volleyball or basketball to start off the semester, when a ping emitted from her computer and broke her concentration. Her gaze flicked down to the e-mail's subject line in the small notification box.

From: Andrew Hodgins

Re: Kimmy Douglas's ballet lessons

Her eyes narrowed and she dropped the pen on the desk, then reached for the mouse. Andrew had agreed to let Kimmy take ballet lessons, so why was he asking about them now? She clicked on the message and her frown deepened.

I'm concerned about Kimmy's grades in mathematics. Her

math teacher would like for Kimmy to attend the study group she offers on Thursday afternoons.

Sam stopped reading and stared blankly at the far wall of her office. Thursday afternoons? That's when Kimmy had ballet classes. She loved those classes. Sam forced herself to finish the e-mail.

As you know, we have to prioritize the student's academic success over their desire to participate in extracurricular activities. Unfortunately, we'll need to pull Kimmy from her ballet classes or find another option. Please schedule a meeting with me to discuss a plan of action.

Sam pushed herself away from the desk, the ergonomic chair rolling smoothly across the scarred vinyl floors of her small office located between the school's gymnasium and locker rooms. Kimmy couldn't quit ballet. She'd only been doing it for a couple of weeks, but Sam could already see how much joy it brought to the young girl. With her parents working halfway around the world, Kimmy was on her own at the boarding school. During a rough patch at Christmas time, the promise of ballet lessons had been the one bright spot in the girl's life.

If there was another ballet class Kimmy could take, Sam would gladly help her switch. Unfortunately, the only other available times would interfere with Kimmy's classes at Bayside Prep.

Sam sighed and pressed her fingers against her temples. She didn't want to have to break the bad news to Kimmy. There had to be some other way to make the current schedule work. She glanced at her computer again, the e-mail from Andrew still glaring at her from the brightly lit screen. Without giving it much thought, she threw on her coat and hat and strode out of the room toward the building where most of the classrooms and administrative offices were located. It was a long trek, as the gymnasium was on the other side of the campus.

When she'd entered the gym that morning, the sky had been dark. Now the sun was high overhead, reflecting brightly off the still-frosty grass that crunched under her feet if she veered off the pavement. Sam passed by the residence hall where she lived and worked as a Resident Advisor—what the kids liked to call a Dorm Mom. Her stomach grumbled, reminding her it was past time for lunch. If only she could be heading inside to eat some of the chili her mom sent home with her on Sunday, instead of marching off to Andrew's office to talk to him.

Sam paused in front of the administration building, flashing back to the day she'd interviewed for her current job. She'd been apprehensive then, nervous about meeting Andrew and interviewing for something that seemed so different from her previous position as a gym teacher at a public high school. Looking back, her main job wasn't all that different now, but the added role as a dorm mother had actually given her the opportunity to get closer to her students. Before, she'd only seen the kids she taught a few days a week for an hour at a time. Now, she got to see them outside of class and be a part of their lives, sharing experiences with them, both good and bad.

Kimmy was one of those students. When Sam had been told that one of her charges was crying in her room over Christmas break, she hadn't known what to do. Although she'd cared for her nieces and nephews in the past, comforting them when they fell down or settling arguments between the siblings, this was a whole other level of responsibility. Here, Sam was basically a stand-in for her students' parents when they weren't able to be there, themselves.

Sam had been proud of how she'd resolved Kimmy's

emotional breakdown, and they'd formed a bond over a shared love of ballet. Now Andrew wanted to take ballet lessons away from Kimmy? Sam gritted her teeth. That wasn't going to happen. She had to come up with something to make Andrew change his mind.

She rushed through the doors of the administration building and into the school's office.

"Is Andrew in?" she asked the receptionist.

The older woman looked up from her computer screen and blinked at Sam, then turned around to glance at the closed door behind her. "You just caught him before his next meeting. Go ahead if he's available."

Sam went around the receptionist's desk and rapped on the door, remembering at the last minute to remove the multicolored knit cap her mom had made her for Christmas. She smoothed her hands over her hair and hoped she looked presentable enough.

She could just make out Andrew's words, partially muffled by the solid wood door. "Come in."

Sam swallowed hard and opened the door. Part of her had hoped he wouldn't be in so she could wait to confront him, but a bigger part of her was glad to get it over with. Normally, she tried to avoid conflict, but this was too important to put off.

Andrew looked up from some papers on his desk and smiled at her. "Sam. Good to see you. I take it you're here about Kimmy Douglas?" He darted a glance at the clock on the wall behind her, then gestured to a chair across from him. "Have a seat."

She perched on the edge of the chair, fighting against the urge to run out of there. "I figured it would be better to talk with you in person." She took a deep breath and let it out slowly. "I thought we agreed that ballet lessons were important for Kimmy's social and emotional development."

He nodded. "They are. But her schoolwork is more important. Her parents have made it clear that they don't want her grades to slip."

"I know, but she loves the lessons. Isn't there anything else she can do to bring up her grade in math?" She forced herself to meet his gaze.

He folded his hands in front of him on the desk and offered her a sad smile. "I wish there was another option too, but the private tutoring schedule is full right now. Unless an opening comes up for tutoring, her math teacher's Thursday afternoon study group is the best plan we've got."

Sam stared at a point on the wall just behind Andrew, her mind racing. There had to be something she could do to make this work. Inspiration struck, and she abruptly turned her focus toward him. "What if I tutor her in math?"

His left eyebrow rose. "You want to help her with math? Do you have time with your other duties on campus?"

She mentally reviewed her commitments. Between coaching the girls' basketball team, teaching P.E. classes, and her role as a dorm mother—not to mention the ballet classes she took at the Riverside Dance Studio, herself— her time was stretched pretty thin. But this would only be a few hours a week, and Kimmy was important. She lifted her chin and looked directly at him. "I can do it."

He peered at her for a moment, then nodded slowly. "Okay. We can try this out until the end of the month, but if I don't see an improvement in her math grades, we'll have to figure something else out."

Relief flooded through Sam, and her words came out

in a torrent. "Thank you, Andrew. This is going to work, I'm sure of it." She stood, surprised by an unexpected urge to walk around the desk and give him a huge hug.

As though he sensed what she was thinking, he rose from his chair and walked around the desk. She stiffened, but instead of pausing in front of her, he grabbed a folder from the top of the two-drawer file cabinet along the wall and opened the office door. "I'm glad we were able to come to a resolution that will benefit Kimmy. I have another meeting now, but if there's anything else you'd like to discuss, please let me know."

He waited for her to exit, then closed the door behind them. Andrew stopped at the receptionist's desk and Sam continued out the door. The brisk air stung her skin as soon as she left the warm administration building, but she was so lost in thought that she barely noticed. Since she'd arrived at Bayside Prep, her interactions with Andrew had been all over the place. Sometimes he appeared standoff-ish, and other times he was friendly. She never knew what to expect from him.

This time, however, she was putting their meeting in the "Win" column. Kimmy's ballet classes were safe—for now. Math wasn't Sam's forte, but how difficult could fourth-grade math be?

5

Jessa

"Go ahead." Jessa stepped out of the aisle after retrieving her carry-on from the overhead compartment to allow an elderly man and his wife to go ahead of her. She was likely the only one on this very full flight who wasn't worried about getting off the plane as quickly as possible.

Landing at SeaTac Airport had completed the last major leg of her journey to Seattle from the Army post she'd been stationed at in Germany. When she'd boarded the first flight, she'd been both excited and anxious about seeing her family again, as well as re-adjusting to civilian life. Now, she found herself dragging her feet.

It wasn't that she didn't want to see Shawn or her father. It wasn't even apprehension about meeting her grandmother, Celia, for the first time. Her hang-up was the secret she'd kept from them for much of the last year.

"Ma'am?" A uniformed flight attendant stood in front of her with a concerned look on her face. "Are you okay?"

Jessa shook her head slightly and smiled at the

woman. "I'm fine. Just got caught up in my thoughts." She stepped out into the aisle and extended the handle on her sensible black rolling suitcase. "Have a nice day."

"You too," the flight attendant said. "I hope you enjoy your time in Seattle."

Jessa forced a small smile. "Thanks." She quickened her pace down the carpeted aisle to catch up with the nearest passenger, who was about to exit the plane.

Once on the jet bridge, she slowed again. Sloping floors had a tendency to disorient her, and she didn't want to fall and cause a scene in the airport. It didn't matter if she hurried, anyway. Shawn thought she was coming a couple of days later, so there wouldn't be anyone waiting to pick her up. She'd planned to catch a shuttle to a hotel in Tacoma so she'd be close to the Army hospital for her doctor's appointment the next day.

The trip to the hotel was shorter than expected and surprisingly uneventful. She grabbed a light dinner in the restaurant attached to the hotel, then turned in for the night. Between the unfamiliar bed and the anticipation of the news she'd receive at the doctor's office that could change her life, she slept fitfully.

When the alarm clock on the nightstand blared at six AM, she slapped her whole hand on the button to shut it off. Even after ten hours in bed, jet lag and a general inability to sleep had left her groggy. She rose slowly and padded to the bathroom, where she washed her face and filled the coffee pot's water reservoir. Soon enough, she'd be caffeinated and semi-awake.

An hour later, a rideshare service dropped her off in front of the wide, sliding doors of the hospital on base. She stepped out of the car and faced the tall building, catching a glimpse of her reflection in the glass. She usually wore her shoulder-length, dark-brown hair in a bun for work, but had left it down today. It framed a face too pale for her liking, with lips pressed firmly together and dark half-moons showing under her eyes. She took a deep breath, then stepped through the automatic doors. A faintly antiseptic odor permeated the air, and she winced, stomach churning. She was reminded painfully of visiting her mother in the hospital before losing her to cancer, and more recently of her own negative hospital experiences.

A couple of hours later, Jessa returned to her hotel room. She flopped onto the king-sized bed and stared up at the smooth ceiling. The doctor's recommendations for a treatment plan had been about what she'd expected, yet it still felt like her soul had been crushed.

Like everything else she'd faced in life, she'd meet this challenge head-on—but she wasn't looking forward to telling her brother.

The next day, Jessa parked her rental car in the gravel lot at the Inn at Willa Bay, removed her luggage from the trunk, and slowly dragged it toward the main building. She stared up at the stately mansion, struck by its beauty. Shawn had told her about the renovations they'd made at the resort, but his description hadn't done justice to the enchanting Victorian-style building with its round turrets and wraparound porch.

An elderly woman opened the front door and stepped out on the porch, leaning on a wooden cane for support and shading her eyes to peer at the visitor.

Jessa stared at her for a moment, taking in her appearance. The woman wore her hair short, in tight white curls nestled against her scalp. Jessa's mother hadn't lived long enough for her hair to whiten with age, but if she had, Jessa was sure this is what she would have looked like.

The older woman's eyes widened. "Jessa? Is that you?" Her hand slid down to cover her mouth.

Jessa's heart hammered. "Celia?" Was that right? Did she call the woman Celia...or Grandmother? Until a year ago, neither Jessa nor Shawn had even known about their grandmother's existence. They'd spoken via video chats, but it was nothing like being a mere six feet away from the woman who'd given birth to Jessa's mother and then vanished from her life.

Celia nodded and Jessa left her suitcases on the side-walk to meet the elderly woman at the top of the stairs, stopping about two feet away from her.

"Oh, honey," Celia said, wrapping her arms around Jessa. "I'm so happy to finally meet you in person. You have no idea how much I've wanted to see you all these years."

Jessa hugged her and stepped back. "I'm glad to meet you too."

Confusion sprang into Celia's eyes. "But why are you here so early? I thought Shawn was picking you up at the airport this afternoon."

"Uh, I caught an earlier flight and decided to surprise you." It wasn't a complete lie. The flight in question just happened to be a couple of days earlier. "I hope it's not a problem?"

"Of course not." Celia squeezed her arm. "We're delighted to have you come for a visit." She eyed her cane ruefully. "If I could handle that much travel, I'd have flown to Germany to see you much sooner."

"No worries." Jessa smiled at her. "I needed to see my dad and Shawn anyway. It's been a few years."

Celia reached for her hand. "Come inside and I'll show you your room and give you the grand tour."

Jessa jutted her chin at the suitcases below. "Sure. Let me grab my luggage and I'll meet you inside."

Celia went back inside, and Jessa rolled her suitcases up the ramp at the other end of the porch, then followed through the open door. A blast of warmth hit her as she walked inside.

"It's lovely." Jessa couldn't stop examining everything in the small lobby. Although Celia had sold half of the resort property to Shawn's girlfriend, Zoe, and their friend, Meg, she'd put the other half in trust for Jessa and her brother. It was odd to be a part-owner of a resort that she'd never before seen in person, let alone never having met two of the other owners.

"Jess!" a male voice cried out, just as strong arms circled her waist from behind and lifted her off the ground.

"Shawn, put me down!" she managed to squeak out as her legs wriggled uselessly in the air. Her big brother released her, spun her around, and enveloped her in a bear hug so tight that she worried she might pass out.

"How did you get here?" he asked when he let her go. "I thought I was picking you up later today."

She shrugged. "I rented a car. I thought I'd surprise you."

His grin stretched from ear to ear. "Well, you did." He glanced over at Celia, who was retrieving a key card from the front desk. "Did Grandma show you around yet?"

Jessa shook her head. "Nope, I just got here."

"Shawnie." Celia wagged her finger at him. "Give me a chance." She turned her attention back to her grand-daughter. "We don't have an elevator, but I'm sure your brother would be more than happy to take your things up to your room." She handed Jessa the keycard, then gave Shawn a pointed look while motioning to the bags.

"Of course." Shawn picked one up in each hand and started for the stairs tucked behind the front desk. "What room is she in?"

"205," Celia said. "It has the nicest view."

Jessa followed Shawn up the stairs, gripping the handrail as she climbed the steep steps. When they arrived at the second room on the left, Jessa held the plastic card in front of an electronic reader and opened the door when the light flashed green.

The room was thoughtfully furnished with beautiful antiques, including a polished mahogany armoire. However, the decor was overshadowed by the real star: the view of what Jessa assumed to be Willa Bay. She'd grown up in Tacoma and hadn't spent much time in this part of Puget Sound, but the sparkling blue waves outside her window reminded her of how much she missed living near the water.

While Shawn set her luggage in a small alcove next to a tall highboy dresser, Jessa crossed the room to get a better look at the bay. When she was a few feet away from the window, her left leg started tingling in an all too familiar manner.

She groaned inwardly. Why now? Her eyes darted to her brother, who was still immersed in the task of arranging the suitcases. She quickened her pace. If she could just get over to the window, she could use it as a brace when her leg inevitably gave out.

She'd almost made it when the room started to spin and her leg buckled. Before she could hit the floor, strong arms lifted her to her feet and steadied her.

"Are you okay?" Shawn asked, still holding on to her. "You looked like you were going to nosedive into the carpet." He chuckled. "Kind of like when we were kids, and you tripped on that gopher hole and got mud all over your new Easter dress. Man, Mom was so mad."

She bit her lip and glanced out the window, hoping that her silence would be enough, and he'd stop worrying about her.

He peered at her more closely. "Seriously though, are you okay?"

She laughed nervously as she surreptitiously tested her stability. Finding that her leg had regained strength, she stepped back. "Oh, you know me, I'm just clumsy. I must have tripped on the carpet."

His expression was full of doubt, but he didn't say anything when she continued toward the window. She examined the property from the high vantage point and let out a low whistle. "It's gorgeous."

Next to her, Shawn beamed at the praise. She wasn't exaggerating for his benefit though. Below them, oyster-shell paths wound their way through manicured green lawns and carefully tended shrubbery. The pièce de résistance was the gleaming white gazebo overlooking the bay.

Jessa had seen the "before" pictures of the resort, and this looked nothing like those. Her brother hadn't even been back in Washington for a whole year, but he and the other owners had really made something of the whole property. It was no wonder that it was now a successful and highly sought-out vacation destination and wedding venue.

A wave of vertigo swept through her brain, and she clutched the windowsill.

"Are you sure you're okay?" Shawn leaned closer to her. "You don't look so hot."

She managed a wan smile. "I'll be fine. I have jet lag,

and I probably need to eat something. You know how bad airplane food is."

"Hmm..." He wouldn't take his eyes off of her. "If you say so." He steered her over to the bed and gently pressed on her shoulders until she was sitting on the floral comforter. "I was going to take you around and have you meet Zoe and some of our employees, but it looks like you might do well with a nap. Grandma made a big pot of chicken and rice soup for lunch, so I'll have someone bring a bowl to you. We can get together later when you're feeling more up to it."

Jessa wanted to protest, but a nap *did* sound good, and homemade soup would really hit the spot. "Thanks."

"I'm really glad you're home, even if it's only for a short time." Shawn leaned down and lightly kissed the top of her head before leaving the room.

Jessa gave herself a few minutes to get her bearings, then got to her feet. She took pajamas out of the larger suitcase, removed a plastic bag full of copper-colored medicine bottles from her carry-on, and brought both items into the bathroom. She changed her clothes, then swallowed a pill from the largest container, washing it down with a swig of water from a drinking glass she found on the counter.

A knock sounded on the door. "Room service," the voice called out.

She walked toward the entrance and called through the door. "Thanks. You can leave it outside. I'll get it in a minute."

Her pajamas may have been modest flannel button-downs that covered her adequately, but there was still something weird about having a stranger see her in them. She checked the peephole. The coast was clear, so she opened the door and retrieved a black plastic tray containing a covered ceramic bowl, a spoon, and a package of Saltine crackers.

She set the tray on the small table near the window and sat down in the chair next to it. A cloud of steam escaped the bowl as she lifted the lid, and she breathed in the tantalizing aroma, hoping it tasted as good as it smelled. She could get used to having a newfound grandmother who could cook.

The soup didn't disappoint, and Jessa devoured it before an overwhelming fatigue forced her over to the bed, where she crawled under the covers for a long nap. It had been an exhausting day, and while she didn't like deceiving her loved ones, she was grateful that she hadn't been pressed into disclosing the real reason she was in Willa Bay.

6

Debbie

"Here you go." Debbie's eldest daughter, Libby, set a freshly brewed cup of coffee in front of her, then sat down at the dining room table with a full-to-the-brim mug of her own. Libby peeled the red lid off of a Tupperware container, revealing four neat stacks of rectangular bar cookies. She held the plastic tub out to Debbie. "Do you want one?"

"Ooh. Those look good." Debbie plucked one from the top and held it up in front of her to examine it further. "What kind are they?" The pale, lightly browned surface was studded with chunks of nuts and something else she couldn't quite determine. She bit into it, letting the sweet confection crumble in her mouth.

"They're butterscotch blondies. This batch has pecans in it, but I made a nut-free version for yesterday's bake sale at the elementary school." Libby took one out for herself, then replaced the lid on the container and pushed it aside.

"Well, they're delicious. You'll have to give me the

recipe." Debbie set the other half of her cookie bar down on a napkin and peered at her daughter. "How are you holding up?" It had been a couple weeks since Libby's husband had moved to Idaho, and Debbie knew it couldn't be easy for her to single-parent their four kids and still keep up with her work at the catering business. If anyone could do it, though, it was Libby.

Her daughter shrugged and reached for her coffee, wrapping both hands around the ceramic mug and fixating on the liquid inside. Finally, she looked up at Debbie. "I'm fine, I guess. Until Gabe left, I didn't really realize how much he did around the house."

"Is he coming home soon for a visit?" Last Debbie had heard, Libby and Gabe had planned for him to return to Willa Bay about every four to six weeks. Normally, he'd be able to make the nine-hour drive in his car, but snow in the passes during the winter necessitated a flight from Boise to Seattle.

Libby shook her head. "Not for another month or so. He's going to be here for President's Day weekend, when the kids get some extra days off from school."

"Well, I know you have a lot on your plate," Debbie said. "If you ever need some time away from the business, just let me know."

"I'll be fine." Libby gave her a tight-lipped smile that didn't quite reach her eyes.

"I know," Debbie said brightly. "But if there's anything I can do to help, either with the business or with the kids, I'm happy to do so." Even as a kid, Libby's type-A personality hadn't allowed her to ask for help, even when it was obvious to everyone around her that she needed it.

Libby held up the paper calendar they used to schedule their catering jobs. "I didn't realize you'd accepted so many jobs for the next few weeks. I thought

53

you'd wanted to take it a little easier with your fundraiser coming up."

Debbie stared at the month of January. She hadn't remembered booking so many events either, but at least a third of the little squares were covered with client information in her own handwriting. The Addisons had begged her to cater their 50th wedding anniversary after their plans for a 'round-the-world cruise had fallen through. They'd been friends with her mother for as long as Debbie could remember, so she couldn't say no. The Cooper Investments dinner party had been a last-minute addition too, but that had been a referral from a long-time client.

As she mentally reviewed each event on their docket, her stomach sank. There were still so many last-minute details to take care of for the cancer fundraiser she was hosting, which was now only a little over a month away. The Addisons' anniversary party coincided with the appointment she'd made with Zoe at the Inn at Willa Bay to discuss final preparations for the fundraiser. Thank goodness she had her daughter to depend on.

Her insides twisted further. Libby was leaving in June to join Gabe in Idaho and then Debbie would be on her own—unless she finally found that assistant she'd been thinking about hiring. But finding an assistant took time, and, lately, time had been in short supply.

Libby furrowed her brows as she consulted her personal calendar on her cell phone. "I should be able to help with all of these, except the Addisons' anniversary celebration. I'm supposed to help William with a big project for school that weekend." She laughed. "I'm not looking forward to having a volcano explode in my kitchen, even if it *is* only a model."

Debbie took a deep breath. This wasn't good. She'd

only agreed to cater the anniversary party because Libby had said she was free that weekend.

Libby scanned her mother's face. "Is everything okay?"

"Uh-huh," Debbie assured her. "Everything is great." She'd find a way to make things work—she always did.

Libby flipped the paper calendar to February and consulted her phone again. "Oh. And there's a few more days that might be tricky for me, but I should be able to move some things around to make them work."

Debbie glanced at the screen of Libby's phone. Almost every day held an appointment. Libby might often act like a superwoman, but even she couldn't be in two places at once.

"No problem," Debbie said breezily. "I can take care of whatever you can't."

"But what about the fundraiser?" Libby asked. "Don't you need to work on that?"

Debbie waved her hand in the air in an effort to appear nonchalant. "I'm almost done with my preparations." She surreptitiously moved the manila folder containing a mountain of to-do lists under another folder, as though Libby had X-ray vision and could see through the cover.

"Mom, I'm serious. Just because Gabe isn't around to help with the kids doesn't mean I can't still do everything that I used to do. William is old enough to babysit now and our neighbor is usually home if there's an emergency." Libby tapped on her phone, narrowing her eyes at it. She shook her head and set the device on the table. "I can handle having him gone."

"I know." Debbie patted Libby's hand and peered into her face. "But we're partners, remember? At most of these events, only one of us needs to be present."

Libby focused on the paper catering calendar, running

her finger down the dates. "I guess so." She frowned. "I hate dumping all of this on you though."

"That's what I'm here for." Debbie gulped the remainder of the cooled coffee from her mug and stood. "I'm going to get a refill. Do you want one?"

Libby handed her the cup she'd been drinking from. "I could use some more." She rubbed her eyes. "Kaya had a nightmare last night and woke up the whole house with her screaming. As a result, everyone was exhausted and crabby this morning. I barely got the older kids off to school in time."

"I'm sorry." Debbie smiled sympathetically and set a fresh cup of coffee in front of her. "That's rough."

Libby sighed, her shoulders slumping as she took a sip of the hot brew. "It was. Gabe is so good at getting Kaya back to sleep when she's had a nightmare. He's been gone for less than two weeks and I can tell the kids miss him. They've all been a little off—not listening to me when I tell them to do their chores or when it's time to go to bed." She shook her head. "I even got backtalk from William when I told him to do his homework before dinner."

Debbie sat down next to Libby. "That's not like him."

"Nope," Libby agreed. She stared into space, her eyes glistening with unshed tears. "I often have to bug the other kids about doing their homework, but William is usually eager to get his work done so he can go practice basketball in the driveway..." Her voice trailed off and she grabbed a Kleenex from the box on the table to dab at her eyes. "He loved playing basketball with his dad on the weekends. That's always been their thing."

"Oh, honey." Debbie handed her another Kleenex, unsure what to say to make Libby feel better, but she knew she needed to tread carefully to avoid making her feel like she wasn't in control. Her eldest daughter had always been the caretaker of the family, including caring for Debbie herself, during her cancer treatments. Now, Libby needed her—and Debbie would do anything in her power to help, even if it was detrimental to her own plans. "Do you want me to take Kaya and Tommy for a few days so you can concentrate on the older kids?"

Libby bit her lip, considering the offer. "No, I think it's better if we all stay together—for now, at least. I don't want to add another change to their lives, even if it's just a long visit to Grandma's house."

Debbie nodded. "I get it. But it's a standing offer if you ever want to take me up on it. I'm always happy to spend time with the kids." She swallowed a hard lump in her throat. She'd always been really involved with her grandchildren but would barely get to see them once they moved to Boise. Her own eyes started to tear up, and she was grateful that Libby was distracted by the buzzing of her phone just then.

"It's the elementary school." She tapped the phone. "Hello?"

A muffled voice came over the line. Debbie couldn't make out the words, but it must not have been good, because Libby pushed herself away from the table and reached for her jacket. "I'll be there in ten minutes."

Libby hung up and slid the phone into her pocket. "Mom, I'm so sorry, but I've got to go pick up William. Apparently, he shoved another kid on the playground and they're sending him home for the day."

"Oh!" Debbie's eyes widened. "Of course. We can talk about this later. Go get William. I'll get my stuff together and lock up here."

"Thanks, Mom." Libby shook her head and frowned. "I don't know what's gotten into that kid, but I hope he's not going to be like this for the rest of the school year."

She rushed out the front door, leaving Debbie alone in the kitchen.

Debbie rinsed out the coffee mugs and placed them in the top rack of the dishwasher. When she returned to the table, she noticed that in her hurry, Libby had left behind a small stack of papers, including a flip calendar made out of bright blue construction paper. One of the kids, most likely Beth, had written "Days Until Daddy Comes Home" in thick black marker and applied liberal amounts of glitter to it.

Debbie sighed. When Libby had told her about Gabe's move to Boise, she'd made it sound like no big deal. She didn't know whether Libby had truly believed that, but it seemed like this separation wasn't going to be easy for any of them.

7

Sam

"Ugh," Mandy groaned. "I think I ate too many pancakes." She held her stomach and winced.

"I told you to stop after the first stack, just like you asked me to." Sam had eaten a few too many pancakes as well. They both walked more slowly than normal back to the dormitory.

"They were so good though!" Mandy sighed. "The pancake breakfast is one of the few things that can make me get up early on a Saturday."

"Agreed. I tried to convince my sister, Meg, to drive up here in time for breakfast, but she had a commitment at the Inn this morning and can't get here until later in the day." Sam checked her watch and grinned. "It worked out though. She's not supposed to be here for about an hour, so I should have just enough time to go into a food coma for a bit."

"Sounds like a plan," Mandy said.

They entered the dorm's lobby, which was empty except for the front-desk clerk.

"Hey, Lacey," Mandy greeted her.

"Hey." The young woman looked up and rubbed her eyes. She held up a thick textbook. "Do you think you could help me with this history question? I can't find the answer in the book."

"Of course," Mandy replied brightly. She seemed to forget all about her aching stomach as she walked briskly toward the desk.

Sam stopped at the row of mailboxes and reached into hers. She didn't often get mail, and it had been over a week since she'd last checked it. To her surprise, there were a few letter-sized envelopes and a thin book that appeared to have been bound by hand, probably using the school's printing press.

A yellow sticky note on the cover read: *I found it! ~Linda Weatherbee*

Why had the headmaster's wife sent her a book? Sam peeled off the note and held the book up to read the title: "Lucia Davis, Headmistress". A memory from the New Year's Eve party over two weeks prior popped into her head. Andrew had mentioned the existence of a book about the woman whose portrait appeared in the same gallery as those of the past headmasters.

Sam waved at Mandy, who was still flipping through the history textbook. "I'm heading upstairs."

"See you later. Tell Meg I said hi." Mandy turned back to her student and Sam started up the stairs.

Once inside her apartment, Sam dropped the mail on her desk and carried the book over to the armchair she'd positioned next to the window. She covered herself with a purple-and-green floral afghan her grandmother had crocheted for her and opened the book. An hour later, she closed the book, turning to gaze out the window.

Lucia Davis had been an amazing woman. Not only had she been the headmaster's wife, but she'd also taken over for him at the school when he and the assistant headmaster had enlisted in the Army to fight in World War II. She'd had her own dance studio, but she'd shuttered it to take on the role of headmistress for two years. According to the biographer, it hadn't been easy for Lucia to give up her own dream, but she'd felt it was important to keep the school running to provide stability to the students and the community.

What must it have been like to take on that kind of responsibility? Lucia had studied to be a teacher prior to marriage and becoming a mother to their daughter, but that wasn't the same as being responsible for an entire school. While Sam had been concerned about serving as a dorm mother for the younger girls because she hadn't done it before, being the headmistress would have been ten times as intimidating. It must have been insanely stressful for Lucia to balance both single-motherhood and her role at Bayside Prep, all while worrying about her husband fighting overseas.

On the end table next to her, Sam's room-phone rang. She picked it up. "Hello?"

"Hey, Sam, it's Lacey. I wanted to let you know that your sister is down here in the lobby." The school's policy required non-students to check in at the front desk before visiting anyone in the dormitory.

Sam glanced at the clock on the wall and realized an hour had passed since she'd sat down with Lucia's biography. She'd been so engrossed in it that she'd completely lost track of time. So much for that nap. "Thanks. Go ahead and send her up."

"Will do." Lacey hung up her end of the line.

Sam stood and carefully placed the book on the end table, then stretched her arms out wide and yawned. The coffee she'd had at breakfast didn't seem to be doing much, so she hoped Meg was up for a walk to the campus espresso stand.

A knock sounded on her door and Sam shouted, "Come in." She didn't usually lock her door during the day because students often stopped by to chat. She glanced at her reflection in the mirror and ran a brush through her straight brown hair, which had frizzed from being pressed against the recliner while she'd been reading.

Meg breezed through the door and smiled appreciatively at the room. "It looks great in here. I like the new bedspread. And the walls are so much more cheerful with the new paint." She wrinkled her nose. "When you moved in, this place looked like a hospital."

"Have you not been here since then?" Sam mentally reviewed the last few months since she'd taken the position at Bayside Prep. "Didn't you come with Mom and Libby once?"

"Nope." Meg shook her head. "I've been so busy planning the restaurant and traveling down to Seattle for my cooking show. I feel like it's been a long time since I've done anything unrelated to work."

"Huh." Sam grabbed her jacket off a hook by the door and checked to make sure her wallet was tucked into the zippered pocket. "I guess the last few months have gone by in a blur for me too."

Meg's gaze followed Sam, and she raised an eyebrow. "Are we going somewhere?"

Sam laughed. "Oh yeah. I need a jolt of caffeine. How do you feel about grabbing a latté and taking a tour of the campus?" She turned around to look out the window. Still not a cloud in sight. "It's a beautiful day—maybe a little chilly, but at least it's not raining."

Meg shrugged and swiveled back toward the still open door. "Sure. I could use some coffee. Taylor and I were up past midnight last night."

Sam raised an eyebrow at the mention of Meg's boyfriend and gave her sister a knowing look. "Oh, really?"

Meg smirked and slugged Sam's arm as they headed down the stairs and out of the dormitory. "Don't give me that look. We were at the barn, trying to map out the kitchen space. I've still got duct tape glue all over my fingers from taping room borders. I've washed my hands with every soap I can think of, and I still can't get all of it off."

She held up her hand for Sam to inspect. Sure enough, a sticky residue remained on a few of her sister's fingers.

"Remember that orange soap Dad uses when he gets tree sap on his hands? Maybe that would work." Sam had always thought it smelled disgusting, but it definitely worked when nothing else did.

"Hmm. I'll give it a try." Meg wiped her hands on the worn fabric of her blue jeans, as though that simple gesture might remove the gunk. "Anyway, enough about me and my restaurant woes. How are you doing? I haven't seen you since Christmas."

They were passing the administration building, and Sam's attention strayed to Andrew's office window on the first floor. The man had a tendency to infuriate her and much of her stress lately had come from his lack of under-standing of how important ballet was to Kimmy.

"Hey, Earth to Sam." Meg tapped her shoulder.

Sam shook her head to clear it. "Sorry. I was just thinking about one of my students. Remember Kimmy, the little girl I brought to Christmas Eve dinner at Mom and Dad's house?"

Meg nodded. "I remember her. She's about Beth's age, right?" She cocked her head to the side. "Weren't her parents overseas during the holidays?"

"They're in Asia." Sam took a deep breath. It felt good to share her concerns about Kimmy with a neutral party. "She's had a hard time being separated from them, and I think it's good for her to have something fun to do to distract her. I enrolled her in ballet lessons at the Riverside Dance Studio, but the assistant headmaster at Bayside Prep is fighting me on it. He thinks ballet might be interfering with her schoolwork."

"Well, is it?" Meg stepped off the path to face Sam.

"I don't think so." As far as Sam knew, Kimmy only struggled with math, and the tutoring sessions she'd scheduled with the girl were helping with that. In the short time that Kimmy had been taking ballet lessons, Sam had noticed a positive change in the girl's demeanor, and she loved seeing how happy it made her young student. But was she putting too much emphasis on ballet being the answer to Kimmy's problems? No amount of ballet was going to make up for being separated from her parents.

"Okay, then." Meg linked arms with Sam. "Now, where's this espresso stand? I'm getting hungry too. Do they have food?"

Sam laughed. She was still full from the giant pancake breakfast, but she knew Meg could always eat, even if she'd just finished a seven-course meal. "They have scones and stuff like that."

"Perfect."

They shifted over to another path that led toward the outer edge of campus and eventually arrived at the espresso stand. A gaggle of teenage girls were in line in front of them, gossiping about their upcoming mid-winter break plans.

"Where are you guys going for break?" a tall, slender girl with a glossy black cap of hair asked the student standing next to her.

The other girl tucked errant strands of blonde hair behind her right ear. "I think we're going skiing in the Alps?" She shrugged and reached out to accept the paper coffee cup the barista held out to her, then turned back to her friends. "I don't know. My mom keeps changing her mind. We went there last year though, so I think we might go somewhere else this year."

The first girl sighed. "I've heard the skiing in Gstaad is lovely this time of year, but my parents always want to go somewhere warm in the winter, so we're going to a resort in Cozumel."

"Me too!" another girl squealed. "We should compare travel plans."

The last of the students received their drinks and the barista turned to Sam and Meg to get their orders. "Sorry about that," she said. "It's not usually that busy on Saturdays, so I'm the only one here."

"No problem," Meg said breezily. "We're not in a hurry."

The barista shot her a look of gratitude. "Well, thanks for your patience. What can I get you?"

They placed their orders and were soon sipping hot lattés—hazelnut for Sam and salted caramel for Meg, who'd nabbed a blueberry scone as well.

"Do you want to check out the waterfront?" Sam asked. "It's only a few blocks away."

"Sure." Meg grinned. "I meant what I said—I'm not in any hurry. This is a welcome reprieve from my normal life."

They strolled leisurely down tree-lined sidewalks, *ooh*ing and *aah*ing over the stately, early twentieth-century mansions lining the streets nearest to campus.

Meg eyed them with appreciation. "I had no idea Paddle Creek had so many old houses. These are gorgeous."

"You should see the headmaster's house on campus." Despite being here for a few months now, it seemed to Sam that she found a new favorite mansion every time she ventured downtown. Today, a white Victorian with ornate scrolls on a front turret caught her eye. It wasn't hard to imagine curling up with a good book on an upper-level window seat or simply daydreaming while gazing out at the water.

"It's like you're in a whole different world here." Meg didn't take her eyes off of the historic buildings. "These places make Mom and Dad's house look like a dollhouse."

Sam laughed at the thought. The house she'd grown up in and that her parents still owned boasted four bedrooms, two bathrooms, and a family room in the basement—plenty of room for everyone to spread out. If their home had seemed like it had ample room, what would it be like to live in one of these mansions?

Meg turned to her and winked. "I mean, they're not in Gstaad, but they're nice enough."

Sam chuckled. "Where even is Gstaad?"

Meg wrinkled her nose. "Switzerland, maybe?" In a quieter, more serious tone, she asked, "Is it weird being around so many people that come from money?"

Sam considered Meg's question. "I hadn't really thought about it before." Did she think differently about her students because they came from wealthier families than she was used to? A few things did give her pause, like some of the older girls having weekly allowances that were bigger than her paycheck. "I mean, some of the kids are a little spoiled, but they're also here alone. I think most of them really miss their families."

"Do you like teaching at Bayside Prep?" Meg asked.

They'd paused at a crosswalk light, and Sam toed the concrete under her foot. "Most of the time. It's different from Willa Bay High though. The majority of the girls on our basketball team get private lessons, so I'm often at odds with what their other coaches tell them."

"That must be tough," Meg said. The light changed and they crossed over to the boardwalk above the public marina. "But do you like it besides that?"

"I think so?" Sam still wasn't sure if she belonged at Bayside Prep, but it was starting to feel more like home. "It doesn't really matter though—I'm only here on a temporary basis."

They sat down on a bench overlooking a dock lined with sailboats.

"Would you take a permanent job if they offered it?"

In front of them, a blue and green sail shimmered in the sunlight. Sam stared at it, her stomach twisting. "I don't know." Something about teaching at Bayside Prep left her feeling unsettled, and she wasn't sure if it was the lack of permanency of her position, or if it was something else. Was teaching at a private boarding school something she wanted to do for the rest of her life?

8

Andrew

Andrew flipped to the final page of the school board's proposed initiatives for the next quarter. He scanned it quickly before setting the thick document on his desk. Leaning back in his chair, he rubbed the lenses of his eyeglasses with the microfiber cloth he kept in the middle desk drawer, then put the glasses back on. He stared at the clock on the wall. Normally he'd head home to his small, off-campus apartment around this time of the evening. Tonight, though, he had a phone call to make.

He sighed and rolled the chair closer to the desk, then double-checked the latest e-mail he'd received from Kimmy Douglas's parents. As he'd thought, they were currently in Hong Kong, sixteen hours ahead of his time zone. If he'd calculated correctly, it should be around ten in the morning there. He dialed their phone number and waited.

After a few rings, a woman answered. "Hello?"

"Hi, is this Jana Douglas, Kimmy's mother?"

"Yes. Is everything okay with Kimmy?" Her voice was tinged with concern.

"Kimmy is doing great," he answered quickly. This wasn't the first time he'd called a parent and had them expect bad news when they recognized the school's phone number. "But there *is* something I wanted to talk with you about. Is this a good time?"

Jana hesitated, and he heard rustling, like she'd settled into a chair. "Now is fine, but I have a hard stop in fifteen minutes. What can I do for you?"

"I'm calling because Kimmy's math teacher noticed she's been having some difficulty with the concepts they're currently learning." His glasses tilted forward, and he shoved them up to the bridge of his nose. When he'd initially talked to Kimmy's parents about their daughter taking ballet lessons, they'd expressed concern about the potential for it to interfere with her study time. He held his breath as he waited for Jan's response. This was exactly why he'd had reservations when Sam had proposed ballet classes for Kimmy.

"Okay..." She said slowly. "Do we need to hire a tutor for her?"

"No, no, nothing like that." He paused, trying to think of the best way to tell her about the conflict with the ballet lessons. He'd promised Sam he'd try to make it work with Kimmy's parents, but a small part of him wondered if he was doing the right thing. Kimmy's difficulties in math weren't currently a major concern, but he didn't want to downplay them either. His own dyslexia had gone undiagnosed in grade school, and he still wished he'd been offered help earlier for the learning disability. Maybe if he had, it wouldn't have caused him so many difficulties later on in life.

Before Andrew could speak, Jana said, "I don't understand why she's having trouble with math now—she's always been so good at it in the past." Her voice rose. "Is it the ballet lessons? Is she spending too much time on them and not enough on her schoolwork?"

Sweat moistened Andrew's palms and he wiped them on his pants. Having difficult conversations with a student's parents was his least favorite part of his job. He cleared his throat. "No, I don't think her schoolwork is suffering because of the ballet lessons. I think she just needs a little extra help with math this quarter."

"Can the school provide that?"

He hesitated, contemplating whether or not to tell Jana that the ballet lessons conflicted with the study sessions taught by Kimmy's actual math teacher. Ordinarily, he'd avoid any chance of upsetting a parent. However, Sam had assured him that allowing Kimmy to stay in ballet lessons was the best thing for her.

But Sam herself had a full schedule. Could he trust her commitment to her student? In the end, it was *his* job on the line. If he wanted to eventually become headmaster, he couldn't afford to get a bad reputation with the parents. Then again, learning to trust his employees was also a necessary skill for the position.

He took a deep breath, then said, "Actually, Sam Briggs, her dorm mother, has offered to help her with her math lessons."

"Oh. I would have expected it to be her math teacher."

"Ms. Briggs is well-qualified to tutor Kimmy and I'm certain she'll be able to help her understand the subject matter." Although his words were firm, he had to force himself to loosen his grip on the phone.

"Well, if you think it will be okay, we'll trust your judgment." Her voice softened. "Kimmy speaks so highly of

Ms. Briggs and I'm sure she'll enjoy spending more time with her."

"Yes, we're lucky to have her here this year." An image of chatting with Sam at the New Year's Eve party popped into his head and the tension eased from his body. If Sam thought she could help Kimmy with her lessons, he believed her. On the other end of the line, Jana was quiet, so Andrew said, "That was the only thing I needed to talk with you about. As I've said before, Kimmy is a lovely student, and we enjoy having her at Bayside Prep."

"I'm glad to hear that," Jana's voice was warmer now, but held a touch of sadness. "It's so hard to be away from Kimmy for so long."

"I can't imagine." It seemed like Jana wanted to continue, so Andrew didn't say anything else.

"We're trying to wrap things up here, at least by the end of the year. When we're settled in our new place, we should be able to have Kimmy come and visit more often. We'd like to eventually find a stable home where we can all live together and Kimmy can attend school near us." She sighed wistfully. "But that's going to be a few more years."

Andrew tried to lighten the mood. "Well, until then, she's part of our Bayside Prep family and we're happy to have her here."

"She does seem to like it." Jana sighed again, then said, "I've got to head out to a meeting, but thank you for calling Mr. Hodgins."

"Of course," Andrew said warmly. "In a few weeks, I'll e-mail you with an update on Kimmy's progress in math, okay?"

"Sounds good. I'll talk to you later." Jana ended the call, and Andrew pushed his chair back from his desk.

Her reaction hadn't been as bad as he'd expected.

Some of the parents were extremely concerned with their children's grades and how they were doing in school—often at the expense of their child's overall wellbeing. It was refreshing to see that Kimmy's mom was willing to attempt to correct the issue without sacrificing the extracurricular activity her daughter loved.

He signed out of the computer, packed up his briefcase, and locked the office door, grabbing his jacket from the coat rack in the lobby. On the way to his car, he called Sam to let her know about Kimmy's parents' decision.

It rang twice before Sam answered. "Hello?"

"Hi, Sam?" he asked. "This is Andrew Hodgins." Although he had contact information for all of his staff in his own address book, he'd never called her from his personal cell phone before, so it was likely she wouldn't recognize the number.

"Oh, hi." She still sounded as though she didn't know what to expect from his call.

"I was calling to let you know that I cleared your plan with Kimmy's mother. As long as you are willing to tutor her in math—and she makes improvements—she can continue to take ballet lessons."

"Oh, that's such great news!"

He could practically picture the relief on her face as she'd been really worked up about Kimmy's welfare when she was in his office the week before. As he neared his car, he tapped a button on the key fob to unlock it, then stuck the briefcase on the passenger seat before sitting down behind the wheel.

"Um, is there anything else I should know?" Sam asked. "Do I need to report her progress to you or anything?"

"Nope." He pushed the Start button and the engine came to life. "Her math teacher is going to let both you and I know how she's doing in two weeks, and we'll go from there."

"Okay, good. That should give Kimmy and I enough time to get into a rhythm with the tutoring schedule." She paused, then said, "Thank you for making this work, Andrew. I owe you."

A warmth swept over him. In his role as assistant headmaster, he often worked hard behind the scenes, and it felt good to have someone—especially Sam—formally recognize his efforts. Over the last few weeks, he'd seen her go to bat for her students and he knew she cared as much about her work responsibilities as he did. "Of course. I'm just doing my job. I want to do what's best for Kimmy."

"I know," she said. "But I still appreciate your help. I felt so bad when she didn't get to see her parents for Christmas, and it was so wonderful to see the change in her when I mentioned taking ballet lessons. She really loves it there."

"I'm glad." He wanted to keep talking to Sam, but he didn't know what else to say. "Well, um... I guess I'll talk to you later. I'm glad we got things settled."

"Me too. Good night, Andrew."

After she'd hung up, he backed his car out of the parking spot and drove the few miles to his apartment on the outskirts of town. He hadn't been to the grocery store in a while, so he pulled a TV dinner out of the freezer and heated it in the microwave. When it was done, he sat down to eat at the small kitchen table, where he spread out the board's proposal in front of him to review a second time. It had been a long day and his work wasn't done yet, but knowing he'd resolved the situation with Kimmy and Sam, made it feel like the day was already a success.

9

Libby

Steam rose from the kettle's spout and a shrill whistle filled the kitchen. Libby turned off the gas burner and poured the boiling water over the tea leaves she'd recently picked up from her favorite tea shop in Willa Bay. Within a minute, the scent of apple with a hint of chai spices wafted through the air. She let it steep for another minute, removed the tea strainer and discarded the used leaves in the compost bin. Then, she carried her drink into the living room, where she sat in the recliner and kicked up her feet.

Her first sip was tentative. Not every tea she'd tried had been a hit, but the sweet apple with a kick of spice was perfect for the mid-January evening. She blew on it and took a few more sips, then set the China cup down on an end table and leaned back in the chair. It had been a long evening. The kids hadn't been too badly behaved, but trying to do dinner, homework, and nighttime chores with four kids was tricky. Now, with the dinner dishes in the dishwasher, the little kids in bed, and William playing on his tablet in his room for another hour, she could finally relax.

As if on cue, the phone rang. She expected it to be Gabe, but was mildly disappointed when she read the caller ID. She tapped the phone to answer the call. "Hi, Miri."

Libby had known Miri Rosenbaum since high school, but they'd become friends again over the past school year after volunteering as room mothers together for their daughters' third-grade classroom. Miri was a top-notch real estate agent, and Libby had thought of her immediately when she and Gabe made the decision to sell their house.

"Libby, hi," Miri said brightly. "I was calling to follow up on the conversation we had about selling your house a few weeks ago at the January birthday celebration in the girls' class. Is this an okay time to chat about it?"

Was it a good time? Libby listened for the kids, but the house was quiet. Despite knowing they'd be moving to Idaho to be with their dad at the end of the school year, the idea of leaving their family and friends behind in Willa Bay was a sore spot, so she tried not to talk about it too much while they were in hearing range. "Now's good."

"Well, I just wanted to see if you were still interested in selling your house. Do you know when you might want to put it on the market?"

Libby's stomach churned and the tea suddenly smelled a little too sweet. She'd known this conversation was coming, but she hated the idea of selling this house. They'd brought their babies home from the hospital to this two-story Cape Cod, and they'd planned to grow old together here.

"Libby, are you still there?" Miri asked.

"Yes, sorry." Libby took a deep breath. "We'd like to move just after school is out, but I'm not sure how long it'll take to sell. That's one of the things I wanted to talk to you about."

"Of course. I hope you don't mind, but I actually took the liberty of driving by your house, and I looked up its details on the county website. It's a beautiful property."

"Thanks." A lump formed in Libby's throat and she swallowed a few swigs of lukewarm tea to wash it down. "I knew it was the right place for us the moment I saw it." A memory flashed into her mind of the first time she and Gabe had seen their future home. She'd been expecting William at the time, and her feet and hands were swollen after hours of house-hunting, but when they'd set eyes on this one, all of the discomfort had faded. They had strolled down the front walk hand-in-hand, whispering to each other how perfect the five bedrooms would be for the large family they planned. And they'd been right—it had been a wonderful house for them. Soon, though, it would belong to someone else. Libby blinked back tears.

Miri's bright voice broke into Libby's reverie. "I'm not sure how much you know about the current housing market, but houses are selling quite rapidly, and I know yours will be no exception. I think we can safely list it in April. If it sells within the first few weeks, we can always include a contingency for the sale not to close until June."

"Sounds good." Libby heard a door shut down the hall —one of the younger kids was still awake.

"Can we schedule a time for me to walk through the property, maybe next week?" Miri asked. "I'd like to get a feel for the interior and see if there are any touch-ups needed before we list it."

"Sure." Libby gave her a few dates, and they worked out a time for Miri to come by while the kids were in school. Libby was already mentally cataloging everything that needed to be done, from the minor items like getting the rest of the crayon off of the wall outside of Kaya's room, to the bigger items like replacing the oven which was on its last legs.

"Oh, and before I go," Miri said, "is Beth going to be able to attend Jenny's birthday party in two weeks?"

Shoot. Libby had seen the invitation come home in Beth's backpack, but with everything going on, she'd forgotten to RSVP. "She wouldn't miss it. Sorry I didn't let you know earlier."

"No worries," Miri said breezily. "Jenny will be thrilled to have her there." She sighed. "She's really going to miss Beth when you guys move. They've gotten to be such good friends this year."

"I know. I feel bad about ripping the kids away from all of their friends." Libby had been so proud of Tommy for going out of his comfort zone and making new friends this year. William would be leaving the best friend he'd had since preschool. Her youngest daughter, Kaya, would not be starting kindergarten at the same school that her siblings, as well as her parents and many of her relatives, had attended. This move would be tough for all of them.

"But you'll be back for the holidays and summer vacations, right? You have so much family around here."

"Definitely." Libby jutted out her chin. "We plan to visit Willa Bay as much as we can. The kids are close with their grandparents, and I don't want them to lose that bond."

"That's great," Miri said. "Well, I'll let you go. I think I hear Jenny and Carrie arguing in their room. Those girls... They'd be awake until midnight if I let them."

"I know what you mean." William was the same way. They'd recently pushed out his bedtime to allow him some freedom after the younger kids were in bed. "I'll see you next week."

After they'd disconnected the call, Libby downed the rest of her tea, noting that it tasted an awful lot like spiced apple cider when cool. She set the porcelain cup near the sink to wash by hand later, then checked on Kaya and Tommy to make sure they were asleep. Both of them were out cold, their little faces relaxed with sleep, and their arms wrapped tightly around their favorite stuffies.

When she opened Beth's door, though, her oldest daughter was lying in bed with her eyes wide open.

"Hey, sweetie." Libby walked across the dimly lit room and sat down next to her daughter's still form. "You look like you're having some trouble sleeping."

Beth nodded and her eyes filled with tears. "I can't sleep."

"Did you have a bad dream?" Libby brushed her hand over Beth's silky hair and the little girl pressed her face into Libby's palm for a moment.

"I heard you talking on the phone when I got up to go to the bathroom." Beth bit her lip.

"Oh?" Libby paused, giving her daughter the space to finish her thoughts.

"I don't want to move." Her lips quivered and fat tears spilled out of her eyes.

"I know, sweetie." Libby gathered Beth into her arms and squeezed her tightly. The girl's tears dripped onto Libby's cotton T-shirt and formed a wet patch, but Libby didn't budge.

"I'm not going to have any friends in Idaho."

"You're going to make lots of new friends. You're such a fun little girl, and I'm sure all of your new classmates are going to want to be friends with you."

"But no one will come to my birthday party."

Libby's heart stopped. Beth would turn eleven in July, just after they moved away from Willa Bay.

She settled Beth back on her pillow, her daughter's eyes following her intently. "How about if we have a party for you before we leave? That way you can say goodbye to all of your friends here and make plans to keep in touch with them after you move."

Beth sniffled. "Really? I can have my birthday early?"

Libby laughed and tucked the blanket around her. "I can't make your birthday come around any earlier, but I can definitely arrange for you to have an early birthday party." She kissed her daughter's forehead. "Now get some sleep. You've got school in the morning."

"Okay, Mommy." Beth closed her eyes and nestled into her blankets. "Love you."

"I love you too." Libby kissed her head again and then stood. After padding her way to the door, she closed it softly and continued on down the hall.

A thin strip of light shone out from under William's door. She knocked on the door, then opened it slightly and called out in a low voice, "Lights out in ten minutes."

"I know, Mom!" William shot back.

"Love you." She grinned. He'd be a teenager soon, and he was already well on his way with the teenager attitude.

"Love you too."

Her heart melted at his words. Even though he'd stopped calling her Mommy in favor of Mom, he'd always be her little boy. She closed his door and went down the hall to the room she'd shared with Gabe. After getting ready for bed, she found herself staring at the ceiling, much like Beth had done earlier.

Her mind raced with thoughts. Would the kids make friends easily? Would she find friends of her own, or a job she liked as much as the catering company she ran with her mom? Would their current house sell, and what did that mean for buying a new property in Idaho? So much about this move was out of her control, and not knowing what the future held was driving her crazy.

After getting the kids up and off to school the next morning, Libby did a ten-minute online yoga video and then tried to meditate. Her friend Zoe swore by the benefits of meditation, but Libby wasn't convinced. It was hard for her brain to settle, and she spent so many minutes fighting a plethora of intrusive thoughts that she wondered if it was a worthwhile use of her time. However, toward the end, her mind quieted and she was able to achieve something close to peace—or at least enough that, when she opened her eyes, she felt more positive about the day ahead than she had in a while.

Willa Bay Provisions had a party to cater that evening, so Libby showered and drove to the catering office. She and her mom had chosen a complicated dessert recipe for the event, one that Libby had only tested once, and she was looking forward to making it. The lengthy preparation would be a welcome diversion from the stressors in her life.

When she arrived at their catering kitchen, her mother wasn't there yet. There was something luxurious about unlocking the door to the business they shared and having the whole kitchen to herself. Libby started getting ready, humming to herself as she took mixing bowls and ingredients out of the cupboards. This was her happy place. There weren't any guarantees in cooking—there was always the chance that something would be slightly off and the recipe wouldn't turn out correctly—but there were things she could do to mitigate that risk, like carefully measuring ingredients and setting timers for the oven.

A half hour later, Debbie walked in the door carrying their business calendar and her laptop. "Morning, Libby!"

Libby finished sifting the final cup of flour into the mixing bowl and brushed off her hands. "Good morning."

"Do you want some coffee?" Debbie asked as she walked over to the sink. "I was thinking about making a pot."

"Sounds good." Libby consulted the recipe she'd printed out and stuck in her catering notebook. Everything had been added to the bowl, so there was nothing left to do but mix. She finished making the dough and set it aside to rest while Debbie made the coffee.

Libby washed her hands and joined Debbie at the side table where her mom had opened up their calendar. Libby flipped open her planner to her business to-do list. "I've got a few phone calls to make today. I should be able to get them done in between making the entrees for tonight."

Debbie zeroed in on the calendar. "We should be able to bake the cookies for the Logan party today too. That'll save us some time tomorrow." She looked up at Libby. "Who do you need to call? Is there anything I can do to help?"

Libby ran her pen down the sheet of paper, assessing the list. "My main priority is to contact Stacey Wheeler. She'd asked me a few days ago about scheduling us for her daughter's wedding this summer."

Debbie beamed and waved her hand in the air. "Oh! You can cross that off your list. I talked to her yesterday."

Libby stared at Debbie, her pen frozen an inch above the planner. "What do you mean?"

"She sent us an e-mail and I called her back yesterday. I know she's your client, but I didn't think you'd mind since you're so busy."

Libby shoved the chair back and stalked over to the coffee pot, not wanting to let her mother see the tears that moistened her eyes. She'd been talking to Stacey for months about the possibility of catering her daughter's wedding and it felt like the job had been ripped out from under her. It wasn't like she and her mom operated on commission or anything—they each owned half of the business—but Libby took pride in bringing in new clients.

"Honey? Are you okay?" Debbie's voice trembled. "Are you mad at me about something?"

So much for trying to hide how upset she felt.

Libby turned to her mother and gave her a tight-lipped smile. "I'm fine." She gestured to the coffee, which had finished percolating. "Do you want a cup?"

Debbie nodded, not taking her eyes off of Libby. "I didn't think you'd mind. The wedding isn't until July, so you won't be able to be her point of contact for the event. I really thought I was helping by taking it off of your plate."

Her mother's words sliced through Libby like the knife she'd used earlier on a stick of butter. As much as Libby didn't want to admit it, she wasn't going to be in Willa Bay in July. She wouldn't be there for the Wheeler wedding or any of their other summer events. Suddenly, her earlier confidence crumbled, and she was sorely reminded that even her sanctuary at the catering kitchen would soon be a thing of the past.

10

Jessa

At nine AM, someone rapped sharply on the front door of Shawn's cottage. Jessa had been resting on the couch, playing a word game on her iPad, and the noise startled her. She set the tablet down on the coffee table and got up, patting down her hair, which had frizzed up after being pressed against the couch cushions.

It felt weird to answer the door at someone else's house, but she opened it halfway to peek out. Zoe stood on the porch wearing a black woolen peacoat over a dark floral sheath dress. She'd slung an oversized leather bag over her shoulder. Jessa stared at her for a moment. Who dressed up this much on a Saturday morning?

"Hey." Zoe beamed at her. "I was wondering if you wanted to see the resort in action today."

Ah. That explained her attire. Jessa opened the door fully and tilted her head to the side as she listened to Zoe.

"We've got a baby shower today at one PM and then an engagement party in the evening. I thought you might like to shadow me so you can see some of our events while you're here." Zoe waited expectantly for Jessa's response.

"Oh." Jessa thought about it. She'd been back in Washington for a little over a week and had noticed a few things happening around the resort during that time, but she'd steered clear, not wanting to get in the way. Then she'd spent the last weekend with her dad in Tacoma, so she'd missed any big events that had occurred then. Being a part-owner of a business and not having anything to do with the day-to-day operations felt strange, but maybe that feeling would subside if she knew more about how everything worked. It would be nice to see the resort in its full glory. "Sure. I'd love to hang out with you today."

"Awesome!" Zoe's smile grew even wider and had an infectious effect on Jessa, who couldn't help but smile, herself. Jessa hadn't known Shawn's girlfriend for long, but she sensed that Zoe's optimism was exactly what her big brother needed. Zoe looked into the cottage. "Did you have a chance to eat breakfast yet?"

Jessa broke out into laughter. "I did. I was up hours ago." She shook her head. "I may be on vacation, but apparently those early Army mornings are ingrained in me." She looked at Zoe. "I wouldn't say no to another cup of coffee though. Shawn only left me one cup and I didn't want to make a whole new pot just for me."

Zoe wrinkled her nose. "And that coffee he drinks is horrible anyway." She gestured behind her, toward the main guest house. "I'll make sure you get a fresh cup from Celia."

Jessa glanced at Zoe's dress and then down at the jeans and wrinkled long-sleeve cotton shirt she'd thrown on that morning. Although she'd washed clothes at her dad's house, she'd had to pack everything back in her suitcase for the trip back up to Willa Bay, and all of her clothing was in the same state as her shirt. "Should I change into something nicer?"

Zoe eyed Jessa's attire, a look of indecision on her face. "Uh..." Jessa smothered a grin. Zoe was too nice to tell her she looked like she'd dressed straight out of a suitcase.

"I think I have something that might be more appropriate." Jessa swiveled around and strode over to the small hall closet, where she'd hung the black sleeveless jersey dress she'd worn to everything from weddings to funerals for the last ten years. Five minutes later, she'd paired it with a royal-blue button-down sweater, a pair of tights, and black leather ankle boots.

Zoe raised an eyebrow. "I think that's the fastest I've ever seen a woman get dressed."

Jessa shrugged. "It helps if you don't have much to choose from." While she didn't own much clothing in the first place, she'd left over half of her meager belongings back in Germany. Once she chose a place to settle in the United States, they'd be packed up and shipped across the ocean to her. She swung her puffy ski jacket over her shoulders, joined Zoe on the porch, and asked, "What are we up to first?"

Zoe adjusted the turquoise wool scarf she wore around her neck and pointed in the direction she'd come from. "First order of business is coffee, and then we can join the morning staff meeting."

Jessa followed her down the graveled lane, past a few other cottages that appeared to be in the middle of a major renovation. She nodded at the small houses. "Which is yours?"

"That one." Zoe pointed at a cute turquoise cottage with a white door and trim.

"It's adorable." Jessa admired the white vintage wooden chair and poinsettia on the front steps.

"Thanks." Zoe glowed with pride. "It was one of the first cottages to be restored. In fact, I lived here before we even started renovations on the rest of the resort property."

"Oh, that's right. I'd almost forgotten you were already renting a place from Grandma Celia before she had her accident." A year ago, Jessa hadn't even known she had a grandmother in Willa Bay and her lips still caught on the word *Grandma*. She'd only just met Celia in person a week ago but had already come to care for the older woman. She recalled Shawn telling her that when Celia had fallen in her house last spring, Zoe had been the one to discover her and call for an ambulance. Then, when Zoe had tried to locate some of Celia's relatives, she'd stumbled upon Shawn's name and phone number, and a decades-old secret had been revealed—Celia was Shawn and Jessa's grandmother.

Zoe led them across the newly graveled parking lot to the inn, where Celia maintained a residence in the owner's quarters with her little dog, Pebbles.

As she'd done every time she approached the mansion, Jessa marveled at the beauty of the structure and surrounding grounds. Shawn's maintenance team kept the hedges and grass impeccably trimmed, and no dirt dared sully the white paint on the porch steps.

Inside, voices trickled through the glass-paned doors to the living room, where guests were eating a continental breakfast and chatting about their plans for the day. Zoe continued on past the empty reception desk in the lobby and down the hall before leading Jessa into the kitchen.

Most of the resort personnel and owners were already gathered there, drinking coffee before the morning staff meeting. Celia stood at the counter brewing more coffee in a commercial-sized pot. When Jessa entered, she caught Celia's eye and waved at her. Celia grinned, then motioned for Jessa to join the others around the table at the far end of the kitchen.

Zoe whipped an iPad out of her bag and took her place at the head of the table. Instantly, everyone quieted. Zoe informed them of the agenda for the day, made sure everyone knew their roles, and then dismissed them. A few minutes later, only Zoe and her assistant, Tia, remained with Jessa in the kitchen.

"Have you met Tia yet?" Zoe asked Jessa.

Jessa shook her head and held out her hand to the dark-haired woman who was dressed every bit as nicely as Zoe. "I've seen you around, but you always seem like you're flying from one task to the next. I'm Shawn's sister, Jessa."

Tia laughed and shook Jessa's hand. "Nice to meet you. I'm sorry I didn't get to meet you earlier. It's been a little crazy around here this week with a bunch of new-client meetings."

"No worries." Jessa smiled at Zoe. "I haven't wanted to intrude on anyone. You've got this place running like a well-oiled machine."

Zoe scrunched up her face. "I wish that were true, but I'm glad to hear that at least it appears everything's under control. To tell you the truth, we're a little short-handed this week. There's a bad cold going around, and several of our staff members are out sick."

"I could help," Jessa volunteered.

"Nah." Zoe waved her hand through the air. "I wouldn't want to make you work on your vacation."

There was that word again—*vacation*. Jessa hadn't yet worked up the courage to tell anyone that her absence from the Army wasn't temporary. She forced a smile. "I don't mind at all. I was actually a Food Service Manager in the Army, and I have experience working events." She mentally stumbled a bit over using the past tense for her job title, but she didn't think Zoe noticed.

Zoe's eyebrows shot up. "Really? Shawn never mentioned you worked in the event services industry."

"Uh, if you can call the military an event services industry." Jessa chuckled, remembering some of the more formal banquets she'd worked. It was always interesting to see how buttoned-up the guests were when they arrived and how loose they became after being lubricated by alcohol as the night wore on.

"I'm sure you've seen some very interesting events." Tia checked something on her own iPad, then looked up at Jessa and smiled. "And if you're really up for it, I'm sure we can put you to work."

Zoe sighed and gave Jessa an apologetic smile. "I hate to do it, but with Shawn out of town this week, we're even more short-staffed at the resort. Would you mind helping out today?"

"I'd love it. I don't have much going on, especially with Shawn gone." With her own trip to see her dad when she'd first arrived and Shawn visiting a friend in Virginia now, she hadn't seen much of her brother. But there'd be plenty of time for that later, because she didn't have any immediate plans to leave the Seattle area. "What do you need me to do?"

Zoe consulted her list again. "We could use help setting up the big tent and then I need someone to assist the caterers during the party." She shot Jessa a worried look. "Is that okay?"

Jessa put her hand on the other woman's arm and smiled at her. "It's great. I'm happy to help." She uttered a self-deprecating laugh. "Honestly, I was starting to feel a little useless around here." She'd devoted so much of her life to her military career, and her forced medical retirement had thrown her for a loop. She was only thirty-eight. What was she going to do with the rest of her life? *And how much longer was that going to be, anyway?* a little voice in her head chimed in. She fought to tamp down the anxiety welling up in her chest and swallowed hard, hoping nobody would see her distress.

She was in luck. Zoe and Tia were both staring so intently at their tablets that she doubted they'd notice if an elephant stomped across the kitchen floor. Jessa turned away from them and walked over to the counter, where she poured herself another cup of coffee. When her mug was filled to the brim, she leaned against the counter, watching the other women as they both focused intensely on their work.

She could tell how much they loved their jobs. Was this something she would be interested in too? She'd enjoyed her role in the Army, and she *was* a part-owner of the resort, but she wasn't sure she shared their passion for event planning. Still, it was something to consider.

After a few minutes, Zoe looked up and her cheeks flushed. "Oh! Jessa! I'm sorry. I got so wrapped up in things that I completely forgot you were here."

Tia gave Zoe a wry smile and put her iPad away in the shoulder bag she carried. "You? Caught up in your work? Never."

Zoe tried to glare at Tia, but it came out a smirk. "I'm not that bad."

"Uh-huh." Tia picked up her coffee cup from the table and carried it over to the sink, where she rinsed it out and set it on a shelf labeled "staff mugs". She grinned at Jessa. "If you're serious about helping out today, follow me."

Tia led Jessa outside and over to one of the big white canvas tents that had been set up on the lawn a few hundred feet from the main guest house. Although Jessa had seen the structures several times over the past week, she'd hadn't yet seen the interior of one. Tia pulled back the heavy tent flap and motioned for Jessa to enter.

Jessa had assumed it would be dark inside, but fairy lights strung between larger light fixtures hung from metal support bars in the ceiling, bathing the room with a soft, romantic glow. "Wow, this is really quite nice."

Tia chuckled. "I remember being surprised the first time I went inside an event tent too. They look so sterile on the outside, but the inside is whatever you want to make of it."

Jessa surveyed the interior. Round tables had been placed in half of the room, leaving space for a dais and microphone at the front, as well as a rectangular table she assumed was for the guests of honor. But she wasn't there to gawk. She straightened her posture and turned to Tia. "What do you need me to do?"

Tia introduced her to the other staff, several of whom Jessa had seen earlier at the daily briefing. They assigned her the job of arranging tablecloths and place settings, as well as a few other tasks, which kept her busy until the 75th birthday party started in the early evening. She then met Zoe's friend, Libby, and Libby's mother, Debbie, who were catering the event and needed assistance with clearing the tables after each course.

Jessa acclimated quickly to the assignment, similar to those she'd done hundreds of times over her Army career. She carried armloads of plates out of the main tent and into a side tent which served as a food preparation area and bussing station. The night had cooled substantially, and while the pathways were lit by small solar lights, she had to focus to keep her footing.

On her fourth trip out of the tent, a seagull swooped

down out of the darkness to retrieve a bite of bread that had fallen to the ground. Startled, Jessa stepped quickly to the side and her leg gave out from under her. Plates, cups, and silverware crashed to the oyster-shell pathway in front of her as she flung her arms out to catch herself. Glass shattered as it hit the hard ground, its ominous sound echoing in the air.

Libby ran out of the prep tent, still holding a wooden spoon. She dropped it on the ground and knelt by Jessa's side, carefully avoiding the glass. "Are you okay?"

"I think so." Jessa tested her leg, but it wouldn't move. She groaned inwardly. This was going to be hard to explain. By this point, several other people had surrounded them, and her face burned with embarrassment.

"What happened?" Zoe appeared out of nowhere, her face flushed as if she'd dashed all the way across the grounds. "I heard glass breaking and someone shouting." She pointed at Jessa's hand. "I think you're bleeding."

Jessa eyed the cut on her hand. In her concern over the numbness in her leg, she hadn't even noticed that she'd been injured by a shard of glass. Now, her hand stung fiercely and blood dripped from it, staining the white cloth of her borrowed waitstaff uniform. "Oh no." She turned wild eyes to Zoe as Libby calmly requested for someone to bring her a first aid kit. "I'm so sorry. I broke all of those dishes...and this blouse is probably ruined."

Zoe waved her hand in the air. "I'm not worried about any of that." A woman jogged up to them and handed Libby a white box marked with a red cross. Zoe eyed the onlookers. "I think we're okay here. Please return to your workstations."

The staff members scurried back into the prep tent, leaving Libby and Zoe alone with Jessa. Zoe took a flashlight and aimed it at the ground. She put the large pieces of broken dishes into a plastic tub, then swept the smaller pieces into a dustpan before dumping them into the tub as well.

Libby pulled on a pair of vinyl gloves from the first aid kit and dabbed an alcohol wipe on Jessa's cut. She examined it closely with a flashlight. "I think you lucked out. I don't see any glass in there, so I'm going to clean you up and put a bandage on it, okay?"

"Do you have medical training?" Jessa asked. "You're really good at this." Libby's take-charge demeanor and calming tone made Jessa relax a bit.

Libby laughed as she wrapped a bandage around Jessa's arm. "No formal training, but I'm the oldest of three kids and I've got four of my own. It seems like I'm patching someone up at least once a week at home." She peeled away the gloves and stuck them in a small plastic trash bag someone had helpfully placed nearby, then peered at Jessa. "How are you doing?"

Jessa wiggled her arms and legs, happy to find that they all responded properly. "I think I'm okay." She ruefully eyed the stained blouse. "Not my uniform though."

Zoe handed the plastic tub full of utensils and broken glass over to a staff member who'd walked by. "I'm sure it'll come out with some bleach, but I think you should get off of your feet for the rest of the night." She held out a hand to Jessa. "That looked to be quite a fall. Let's see if you can stand."

"Oh, I'm sure I'm fine." Jessa moved into a kneeling position and reached for Zoe's hand. Her legs wobbled as she got to her feet, and she was glad she'd accepted Zoe's offer of help. She stood still for a moment to regain her equilibrium. The cut throbbed under the bandage and

Jessa grimaced in pain. This evening definitely hadn't gone according to plan.

Zoe and Libby exchanged glances and, without asking Jessa for permission, they moved to either side of her and helped her walk back to Shawn's cottage. Both of her legs felt as rubbery as Gumby's the further she walked, and she had to lean on the two women to keep her balance. When they got inside, they deposited her on the couch.

Libby eyed her watch. "I'd better get back to manage the dessert service, but let me know if you need anything else." She turned to Zoe. "You'll stay with her for a while, right?"

Zoe nodded in response. "Tia's got everything under control with the event. We'll be okay here."

Jessa forced brightness into her voice. "I'm totally fine. It was just a silly fall. I have a tendency to be clumsy, but you fixed me up and I'll be right as rain by tomorrow morning. Both of you should get back to the event. Don't worry about me."

Libby bit her lip, as if uncertain whether or not she should leave.

"Go." Zoe motioned Libby to the door. "I'll stay with Jessa, whether she likes it or not." She shot a smile in Jessa's direction.

"See you both later then." Libby stood in the doorway and addressed Jessa. "I hope we have a chance to get know each other under better circumstances before you leave Willa Bay."

"I'm looking forward to it." Jessa managed a weak smile as she leaned back into the couch cushions, suddenly too tired to sit upright. The day had been longer and more strenuous than she was used to, and with the effects of her illness, it seemed like all of the energy had drained from her body.

Libby firmly closed the door behind her, and Zoe pulled a chair over to the couch. She stared at Jessa for a few seconds.

Jessa's skin prickled. "What is it?"

Zoe cleared her throat, then met Jessa's gaze. "Is something going on with you?"

"What do you mean?" Jessa tried not to squirm under Zoe's scrutiny.

"Everyone trips and falls once in a while. That's totally normal." She sighed. "But Shawn told me there was an incident with you tripping over the carpet in your room when you first got here."

"I'm just clumsy."

"You had trouble walking back from the event too. If Libby and I hadn't been there to support you, I don't think you would have made it to Shawn's cottage." Zoe put a hand on Jessa's arm. "Is there something we should know?"

Jessa turned away from Zoe and stared out the window. She hadn't wanted anyone to know about her illness. Most of the time, she could control the symptoms or mask them from other people. Tonight's incident had been worse though, and she wasn't sure how much longer she could hide her condition. She took a deep breath and announced matter-of-factly, "I have a brain tumor. It's why I came home."

Zoe's eyes widened and she inhaled sharply. "Oh my gosh." She was quiet for a moment as she processed Jessa's news. "Shawn doesn't know, does he?"

Jessa shook her head, a movement that took much more effort than it should. "No one besides my doctors and commanding officers know about it. There's an Army surgeon in Tacoma that specializes in these types of tumors, and I met with him when I first arrived in

Washington. He's cleared me for surgery in a few weeks." She looked up at Zoe. "I didn't want all of you to worry about me—to pity me. The doctor seems confident that he'll be able to remove all of it and I should make a full recovery."

Zoe took Jessa's uninjured hand. "I'm glad you told me. You have a lot of family and others here who care about you. We'll all be here for you, whatever you need."

Jessa blinked a few times, and the weight in her chest lessened. Keeping a secret from Shawn and her dad had been burdensome, but it had been even harder to not have anyone to talk to about her illness. "Thank you. I appreciate it." She squeezed Zoe's hand. "Can you keep this to yourself until Shawn is back from the East Coast? I'd like to tell him in person."

"Sure. I won't say a thing to anyone until I get the okay from you." Zoe smiled at her. "But maybe take it easy until after your surgery. From what I've heard from Shawn, you haven't taken a vacation in years. This is a great reason to take some time off and spend time with your family. Learning about the Inn's operations can wait. Besides, I'd love to show you around Willa Bay and get to know you— if you'll let me."

"I'd like that." Jessa gave Zoe a weak smile, then she finally let her eyes close.

A while later, she half-woke to the sounds of a chair being pushed under the kitchen table and Zoe's feet tiptoeing toward the door. Jessa had known Zoe was nice, but she hadn't realized how quickly she would come to like her brother's girlfriend. Telling Zoe about her illness had been scary, but it had been worth being vulnerable. Without opening her eyes, Jessa let herself drift back into a well-deserved deep sleep.

11

Sam

Sam was so engrossed in the book about Lucia Davis that she almost didn't hear the insistent melody blaring from her cellphone. Reluctantly, she closed the book and set it on the end table, then slid her finger across the phone's screen to shut off the alarm. She'd had just enough time after her last class of the day to get a quick snack and read a bit before Kimmy's ballet class.

Sam stood and stretched her fingers toward the ceiling, going up on her toes for a minute. Although sore from her own ballet class earlier in the week, she loved how it felt to move her body and she relished every bit of the soreness in her muscles. How had she gone so long without ballet in her life? It seemed like a lifetime ago that she'd made the decision to quit in favor of pursuing other dreams, like college and teaching.

She got ready to go, then grabbed her purse, exited her room, and turned left at the hallway leading to Kimmy's room. As she walked toward the end of the hall, she passed a partially open door and heard Mandy talking to a student in a soothing voice. Sam hesitated, not knowing if she should knock on the door to let her co-housemother know she was leaving. She didn't want to intrude on anyone's personal space though, so she opted to send Mandy a quick text to let her know she'd be off campus for a while with Kimmy. As she moved away from the door, she heard the student sobbing.

It sometimes surprised her that, while it seemed like the girls in her dorm had everything money could buy, they were just the same as any other school-age girls she'd ever met. They still had problems with school, friends, family—and, for the older girls, romantic relationships. Having a generous allowance from their parents may ease some of the strain of being away from their family, but it didn't shelter them from everything.

Kimmy's door was open, but Sam knocked on it lightly as she stuck her head inside. "Kimmy? Are you here?"

Kimmy looked up from her desk and blinked a few times at Sam before glancing at her clock and heaving a sigh that would make a theater actress proud. "I thought it would never be time." She slammed the cover on her math book, shoved it to the back of her desk, and popped up from her chair. "I need to run to the bathroom and then I'll be ready, okay?"

Sam nodded and moved into the room as Kimmy passed by her to go to the communal bathroom down the hall, then Sam glanced at the page of math problems on the desk. Most of them looked correct, but her tutee was still having some issues with multiplication. Still, Sam was happy to report that Kimmy had steadily improved over the last few weeks.

When Kimmy came back, she opened the closet and grabbed a violet duffel bag. "Okay, let's go."

Kimmy chatted animatedly the entire way to Willa Bay. By the time Sam had delivered her student to the ballet teacher, she was mentally exhausted. She didn't like to leave the building for too long while Kimmy was in class, but today she took a quick walk up the hill above Main Street, climbing high enough to see the sun sink deeper into the horizon. Gorgeous purple and pink hues infused the sky, and Sam took a moment to acknowledge how grateful she was for everything in her life. She may not know what her future held, but her present was pretty darn great.

Sam walked back down the hill and opened the door to the ballet studio, her cheeks flushed from the cold and the exertion of her hike. The room felt warmer than before, likely because she'd grown accustomed to the dropping temperatures outside. She unzipped her jacket and dropped it on a chair in the lobby. She'd forgotten to bring her own reusable water bottle, so she walked over to the water cooler and filled a tiny paper cup. A few gulps later, and the cool liquid was gone. She refilled the cup and drained it as well, spilling a third of it down the front of her shirt.

She went into the bathroom and dabbed at her shirt with a paper towel, then came back out into the lobby, wandering over to the bulletin board covered with photos of past and present ballet students, and casts of the various performances throughout the years. As she inspected one of the older photos, hoping to catch a glimpse of her younger self, she heard footsteps behind her.

"It's been a good run, hasn't it?" Tansy Taylor lightly smoothed down the edge of a curling photo with a finger-tip. She gazed with pride at the board. "I'm going to miss this place when I retire."

Her words cut through Sam like a knife. Retire? Sam had just returned to the ballet studio and now Tansy was retiring? What did that mean for the studio? And lessons for both Kimmy and herself? She forced herself to swallow and asked, "Are you leaving the Riverside Dance Studio?"

Tansy nodded, an almost wistful smile forming on her lips. "Not for a few months, but sometime this year."

"But why?" Sam would guess Tansy was around seventy, but she'd always seemed ageless, with her svelte figure and energetic demeanor. Sam took a hard look at the older woman, noticing for the first time the lines in her cheeks and the crow's feet around her bright blue eyes.

Tansy shrugged and turned away from the bulletin board, sweeping her hand through the air. "It's just time for me to move on. My husband retired last year, and he's itching to travel. We haven't been able to do so, though, because I'm tied to the day-to-day management of the studio."

"Are you going to sell the business?" Sam's eyes prickled with tears at the thought of her safe place being turned into yet another gift shop on Willa Bay's Main Street.

"I'm not sure." A thoughtful look came over Tansy's face. "Are you interested in buying it?"

Sam chortled. "Me?" The thought of herself owning the ballet studio was absurd. For one, she was a P.E. teacher, and she already had a job. Not to mention she'd been away from the barre for so long that her ballet skills were rusty, at best.

Tansy grinned as though she'd discovered a new protégée. "Yes, you. You'd be perfect. I know how much you like educating young minds, and I've seen you with Kimmy. Your students love you."

Objections whirled through Sam's mind, and she could barely catch a thought long enough to express it. She finally managed a lame, "But...I'm not a ballet teacher."

Tansy patted her on the shoulder. "You don't have to be. I have a few teachers on staff, and they're always wanting more hours. Whoever takes over the studio would need to have a love for ballet and a desire to see their students succeed, whether that be progression in their abilities or simply enjoying the activity."

Sam's head cleared enough that she could see Tansy's proposition was impractical. She needed a secure job with a steady paycheck—the exact opposite of what Tansy was proposing. "I don't see how I could make it work. I couldn't afford to buy the business from you, and, quite frankly, I have no clue how profitable a ballet studio could be." She shook her head. "I appreciate you thinking of me, but I don't think it's possible."

Tansy studied her, the smile not wavering from her face. "Why don't you think about it for a bit and get back to me."

Sam pressed her lips together, then nodded. She hated to dash Tansy's hopes, but in her heart, she knew it wouldn't work. Her future career might not lie with Bayside Prep, but she didn't think it was here at the ballet studio either. "I'll think about it." She walked over to the glass window to view Kimmy's class and Tansy followed.

They watched as the instructor demonstrated a pose and the girls did their best to imitate it. Kimmy had only been in the class for a few weeks, but she arranged her body into the position just as well as the other students. A rush of pride swept through Sam. Although Kimmy had been excited about taking ballet, Sam hadn't been sure if her enthusiasm would be short-lived once she actually took a class. She was pleased to see that Kimmy was taking it seriously and seemed to love it. It seemed crazy to think that only a month ago Kimmy had been crying in her room, and Sam had cheered her up by introducing her to a few beginning ballet positions. Watching her now was a good reminder that Sam was making a difference in her students' lives, even when it didn't feel like she had much influence over them.

Sam turned to Tansy. "How do you think Kimmy is doing?"

Tansy grinned. "She's doing great. Her teacher says she's picking up poses quickly and is determined to catch up with the girls in her class who've been taking lessons for much longer. She's got that 'can do' spirit." She eyed Sam pointedly and added, "Much like another girl I once knew."

Sam took a deep breath and released it slowly, her eyes trained on Kimmy. "I wish I still knew that girl too." That utterance felt like a betrayal of the life she'd built, but there was something to it. As a child, Sam had been naive about the personal and monetary costs of her dream of being a professional ballerina, but a year of college and being out in the world had quickly given her a dose of reality. She had living expenses to worry about now, and concerns about her future in teaching—and nothing left for the luxury of pursuing a passion project. Not that she didn't love teaching, but it wasn't the same as the love she'd once had for ballet. She found that she missed the girl she'd once been, the girl who'd been convinced that ballet was her future and she'd do anything to make it happen.

The door at the back of the room opened and a group

of girls piled out, giggling like mad as they hopped along on the toes of their sneakered feet. Sam realized that a few parents had entered while she and Tansy were watching Kimmy's class.

Tansy turned to greet them, then looked back over her shoulder at Sam. "Think about what I said, okay?"

Sam nodded. "I will."

12

Andrew

Andrew eyed the brown paper sack he'd retrieved from the office refrigerator and placed on the other side of his desk, then reluctantly reached for it and pulled it toward him. When he stuck his hand inside, he was mildly disappointed that the ham and cheese sandwich hadn't magically morphed into something more interesting. He generally ate the same thing every day, but he'd heard the office manager raving to one of her co-workers about a new food truck down by the marina, and now he craved the paninis and salads she'd mentioned.

Still, though, he'd brought his lunch, so he didn't have a reason to leave the campus. He was known to eat at his desk, barely stopping work to wolf down bites of food, but he'd been working long hours lately and he deserved a break. Staring at the two pieces of tired whole-wheat bread he'd slapped around a few slices of ham and provolone, Andrew was suddenly filled with a strong desire to get out of the office.

He stuffed the sandwich back in the sack, lifted his jacket off of the coat rack and put the bag back in the fridge. As he passed by the front desk on the way out the door, he said to the office manager, "I'm taking my lunch break. I'll be back by two for my meeting with the board."

She looked up at him in surprise. "You're going out?"

Her voice was so incredulous that he knew he'd made the right decision. It was time to shake things up a little, even if he was only being as rebellious as forsaking his customary brown-bag lunch for a meal out. He buttoned his jacket and exited the building, finding a little spring in his step that hadn't been there earlier. He took off down the sanded concrete path leading to the edge of campus closest to Paddle Creek's waterfront. It had snowed overnight, and although more hadn't fallen yet today, the matte-gray color of the sky indicated that the weatherman's forecast of afternoon snow could soon be fulfilled.

When Andrew crossed the campus boundary, he felt a mental shift, almost like permission to forget about work for a while. He slowed his pace and enjoyed the walk through the park bordering the waterfront. As he neared the food trucks in the marina parking lot, he saw a woman sitting on a backless bench under a tree. Her head was down as she hugged her knees tightly to her chest, but he immediately recognized Sam Briggs's colorful knit cap.

If he stayed on his current path, he'd walk past her in a few minutes. Should he bother her? He thought about saying hi, but when he neared her, he noticed her eyes were squeezed shut and her lips were pressed tightly together, as though she were deep in contemplation. Probably better to pretend he hadn't seen her and leave her to her thoughts.

Snow started to fall, and he grinned. Although wasn't the first snowfall of the season, he never tired of seeing the world around him turn into a winter wonderland.

From the corner of his vision, he caught a glimpse of Sam opening her eyes and leaning forward to stick her tongue out to nab a snowflake. A laugh escaped his mouth before he could stop it. Her gaze darted toward him, her eyes widening in surprise, and she snapped back up, smacking her head against the tree trunk.

"Ow." She sat straight up, causing her knit cap to catch on the rough bark. Static electricity made strands of her hair spike outward as she gingerly palpated her scalp. "That hurt." She glared at the tree and started to reach toward it to free her hat, but Andrew stepped forward.

"I'll get it." He gave it a gentle tug, but it stuck insistently. He moved closer and leaned in to inspect it, not wanting to rip the delicate yarn. As he worked on the hat, his eyes darted to Sam. "I'm so sorry. I didn't mean to startle you like that."

He finally managed to dislodge it and handed it to Sam, who rubbed her head one last time, then carefully slid the hat over her long brown hair. She glanced up at him. "No problem. I just didn't hear you until you were right next to me."

He shoved his hands in his pocket and stared down at his feet, then looked at her from the corners of his eyes. "You were so deep in thought that I didn't want to bother you."

"Oh. I guess I *was* a little preoccupied." She pressed her lips together but didn't elaborate.

At that moment, a gust of wind ruffled the treetops, relieving a branch above them of its thick coating of snow from the night before, which immediately blanketed them in a cascade of white powder.

"What the—?" Andrew sputtered, swiping at his face

with his bare hands and scooping snow from his coat collar before it could fall down the back of his shirt. He loved a good snowstorm, but he wasn't so thrilled by this development.

Next to him, a giggle erupted from Sam, and he turned his attention to her. She'd been showered with just as much of the white stuff as he had, and it sparkled like diamonds in her eyelashes. She flashed him a wide grin and he found himself chuckling alongside her.

He glanced upward, now overly aware of the tree's snow-laden branches. "Um, maybe we should get out of here before we're given a full ice bath."

She laughed again, and he noticed that the stress he'd seen earlier on her face had disappeared. "I think you may be right." She got to her feet, tugged on the hemline of her jacket to clear the snow, and checked her watch. "I was sitting here so long that I almost forgot I'd ventured out to get some lunch."

"I was heading over to the food trucks at the marina." He gestured to the path in front of them, then brushed off any remaining snow from his jacket. "Maybe you'd like to join me? My treat. I feel like I owe you for what just happened."

She chewed the corner of her lip and looked in the direction he'd indicated. "I should probably get back. I wanted to take care of a few things before my next class period."

"Can they wait?" As soon as he asked the question, he mentally chided himself. He'd always been extremely focused on his work, and he admired that quality in others.

What had gotten into him? First, he'd skipped out on preparing for the upcoming board meeting, and now he'd impulsively asked one of his staff members to play hooky from her work to eat lunch with him. His heart hammered in his chest.

Her wide eyes reflected both his own surprise and a hint of indecision, but after a moment, she shrugged and said, "I suppose none of it is terribly time sensitive and I *am* hungry."

"Great." He stuck his hands in his coat pockets and nodded toward the marina. "Shall we?"

They walked next to each other companionably for a few minutes. When they were almost out of the park, Sam paused and stared straight ahead. "Oh! I didn't realize there would be so many choices!"

Five food trucks had set up shop in the side parking lot of the marina. People seemed to have come out of the woodwork, milling around and chatting with co-workers and friends. A large tent had been erected on the adjoining grass, and happy customers filled the seats of the plastic picnic tables under the canvas cover.

Andrew and Sam strolled through the parking lot, examining all of the offerings. He wasn't familiar with the food truck scene, but his stomach growled loudly as he read the menus posted outside each of them. Not only was there the panini place the office manager had raved about, but there were also vendors of tacos, falafels, pasta, and crepes.

"What sounds good to you?" he asked. "I'm thinking about the Italian chicken panini, but the Nutella banana crepe sounds good too."

"I haven't had good falafel in a while." She grinned at him. "We could split the crepe for dessert?"

"I'm up for it."

They stood in line at their chosen food trucks, then took their lunches over to the tent, where they found an empty table. Andrew sat after setting their food down and

Sam unzipped her jacket before sliding onto the bench across from him.

She bit into her falafel pita, dropping a glob of tzatziki sauce on the red-and-white-checkered paper basket it had come in. "Oops."

He laughed and unwrapped his own meal. The aroma of oregano and fresh basil permeated the air and he inhaled deeply. He bit into it and sighed. It was every bit as good as he'd been promised. "This is so much better than the ham and cheese I left back in the office." He quickly finished his sandwich and took a swig from the can of Barq's Root Beer he'd bought, then transferred half of the dessert crepe to his empty sandwich wrapper.

Sam seemed to be enjoying her sandwich, but her eyes were unfocused, as though she were somewhere else. He let her eat in peace for a few minutes while he looked around the inside of the tent and sipped his drink. The air buzzed with chatter, with occasional peals of laughter punctuating the din. A smile crept over his lips, surprising him, but even that simple action brightened his spirits. Lately, he'd been so focused on work that he'd almost forgotten the simple pleasure of getting out of the office and having lunch with a companion. He glanced back at Sam, who was dipping her last piece of pita into a smear of hummus that remained on the plate.

"I take it you liked your food?" he asked in amusement as she savored the last bite.

Her head shot up and her cheeks flushed. "Oh, sorry. I was ignoring you, wasn't I?"

His eyes widened. "No, not at all. You just looked like you were working through something, so I figured I'd let you be."

She sighed, and dabbed at her mouth with a paper napkin, which she then crumpled into a ball and dropped into the empty checkered serving basket. She reached for her half of the Nutella crepe and slowly chewed it before saying, "I've got a lot on my mind."

"Do you want to talk about it?" While he waited for her to respond, he pushed his own garbage to the side and neatly positioned the empty soda can next to it.

She shrugged her right shoulder, causing her knit cap to shift on her head. She straightened it, then met his gaze. "I'm just not sure what I want to do next year. I know the job at Bayside Prep is only temporary and I need to start thinking about what comes next." She sighed again and looked out toward the boats bobbing in their slips in the marina.

He leaned forward and rested his elbows on the surface of the picnic table, tenting his hands together in front of him. He'd recently learned that the teacher Sam was subbing for had decided not to return after she concluded her maternity leave. It wasn't like him to make staffing decisions on the spur of the moment, and neither had he spoken to the headmaster about offering Sam a permanent position, but Sam had made a good impression on both students and staff, and he didn't want the school to lose her. He didn't think his boss would have any objections.

"What do you think about staying at Bayside Prep for next school year?"

She cocked her head to the side. "What would I be teaching?"

"You'd have the same position you have now." He quickly added, "If you're interested in it, I mean."

"But what about the teacher who had a baby?"

"Her husband is being transferred to a Naval base on the East Coast in a few months and she wants to go with him." He peered at her. "So, the job is yours if you want it."

She hesitated, and indecision flickered across her face. Her lips moved as if she was about to say something, but then she shut them abruptly and turned her gaze to the gray-blue waters of Skamish Bay.

His heart dropped in his chest. Did she not like working at Bayside Prep? Was it something he'd done? "Of course, I understand if you don't want to stay at the school for next year." His words sounded flat to his ears as his mind raced and he tried to hide the disappointment coursing through his body. His tongue turned to cotton, and he fervently wished that he'd saved some of his soda. He reached for the discarded can, shaking the last drop of liquid into his mouth.

Why was he so upset about Sam not wanting to stay? He had years of experience hiring staff at Bayside Prep and knew that not every candidate would ultimately accept an offer.

"No, no. It's not that," she said hurriedly. Her hazel eyes met his gaze. "It's just that the owner of the dance studio where Kimmy and I take lessons offered to sell me her business."

"Oh!" He hadn't expected her to say that. He straightened his spine and braced his hands against the table edge, pushing himself as far back on the bench as he could.

"Is that a problem?" she asked, her eyes worriedly searching his face. "I'm not sure I'm even interested in buying the business—and even if I was, it wouldn't happen until after my contract here with Bayside Prep is complete."

"No, it's not a problem." He sighed, weighing his options while simultaneously trying to gauge how she was feeling. Sam was obviously under a lot of stress, and he didn't want to add to it by pressuring her to take a permanent position at Bayside Prep. He folded his hands in front of him again and leaned forward. "How are you feeling about the ballet school option? Do you think it's something that would appeal to you?"

"I don't know." Sam drank from her can of berry-flavored sparkling water. "I've always loved ballet and I have fond memories of the studio in Willa Bay, but I love coaching and teaching at a bigger school too. Owning my own business was never really something that I saw for my future." She shrugged and looked past him at the food trucks. "Some of my friends and family are business owners, and it seems so stressful at times."

Andrew regarded her thoughtfully. "I'm sure there are good things about it too. You'd get to manage the business the way you see fit, and you wouldn't have to answer to anyone else."

"Except my students' parents who don't like the way I'm teaching or doing something." Her eyes danced with mirth. "I don't think there's ever an escape from other people's opinions."

He laughed. "If I had a nickel for every time a parent called with a concern about their student…"

"You're never going to please everyone." She smiled at him. "I'm probably way overthinking this. It's not something I have to decide today."

He shook his head. "Nope. But I was serious about the role at Bayside Prep. It's yours if you want it, but I will need to know something within the next month or so."

She bobbed her head vigorously. "Of course. I'll definitely let you know as soon as possible. I do appreciate the offer, and if it wasn't for this ballet thing, I'd jump at the chance to accept it."

"Understood." He pushed himself up from the table and gathered their garbage, depositing it in the trash and recycling bins near where they sat. "I've got to get back to campus for a meeting with the school board, but we should talk more about this later."

Relief flooded her expression. "I'd like that. I have to admit, it was nice to talk to someone about all of this. My family would think I was a little crazy to even consider buying the ballet school."

"Sometimes crazy is good."

She shot him a look of surprise, but didn't say anything. He busied himself with buttoning his wool jacket to cover his own shock. Crazy is good? What had come over him? His life motto had always been to take the safe and predictable path to success. Every major decision he'd made in life had been carefully planned out to the letter.

They walked back to campus along the same path they'd taken to the marina. Snow had continued falling the entire time they'd been under the cover of the picnic area. It hadn't looked like much in the well-traveled parking lot, but at least another inch of the white stuff had accumulated in the park.

Sam lightly touched her fingers to her knit cap when they passed the bench where she'd been sitting earlier. "I think I've learned my lesson about sitting under a tree when it's snowing." At that moment, a breeze swept through the trees, showering them both with icy wetness.

She yelped and blindly jumped backward, running into him. He tried to steady her, but he slipped on the fresh snow on the path and his feet went out from under him. They tumbled to the soft, snow-covered grass, him landing on his back with her against his chest. Slightly stunned, he lay there for a moment, idly pondering how he'd gone from the safety of his office chair to lying on the ground with one of his staff members in the course of an hour.

Sam recovered quickly, bursting into a fit of laughter as she rolled away from him. Her hat had fallen off again and her hair and jacket were coated in snow, as though she'd just attempted to make a snow angel. He sat up and reached for her hat, replacing it firmly over her ears. She quieted and stared at him. For a few seconds, time stood still. They were so close that he could feel her warm breath against his chilled skin.

She broke the spell first, leaning back, grabbing a handful of snow, and flinging it at him. He sputtered and swiped at his face. "Hey!"

She giggled. "Sometimes crazy is good, right?"

He paused, taking in her flushed, smiling face, then laughed and shook his head. "I guess it is." He retaliated by dropping a scoop of snow over her head, making her squeal. An elderly man passed by, giving the two grown adults sitting on the ground and laughing hysterically an odd look and wide berth. The man's reaction only made them both laugh harder as they brushed snow from their hair. When their laughter subsided, Andrew stood, offering his hand to help her up.

She eyed him with mock suspicion. "I don't know if I can trust you."

"Scout's honor, ma'am." He withdrew his hand and gave her the Cub Scout salute. "I promise to be honorable."

Sam grinned and let him pull her to a standing position. She brushed off the snow from her jeans and eyed the wet denim ruefully. "I think I'm going to need to change before my next class."

"Me too." He wrinkled his nose. "This has to be the

most adventurous lunch I've had in a long time." *And*, he thought to himself, *the most fun.* Where had the fun gone in his life? Once upon a time, he'd enjoyed goofing off with his sister or his friends. Now, his idea of a good time was sitting alone in his apartment with a bowl of popcorn and a good movie. What had happened to the person he used to be?

They walked back to campus together, walking close enough that their arms touched occasionally. Sam relayed a story about a time she and her sisters had had an epic snowball fight with some of the neighbor kids, until they reached her dormitory and they had to part ways. He paused in front of her building, thinking about how much fun he'd had with her. It had seemed like there was a spark between them, but had he imagined it?

It didn't really matter. Even if there was something between them, it wasn't appropriate to have such thoughts about someone he worked with—not to mention the fact that he had somewhat of a managerial role over her. Today had been fun, but he'd need to make sure to maintain a professional relationship with Sam in the future. His good mood deflated, and he took off at a brisk pace toward his office.

13

Libby

Kaya's shrieks pierced the relative quiet Libby had achieved with a cheap pair of noise-canceling headphones. Libby looked up from her computer and cocked her head in the direction of the basement door. The shrieking stopped and Libby sent up a silent prayer of thanks. She'd been working on a catering quote for Angela Rasmussen's sixtieth birthday party for the last two hours and hadn't made much progress.

Normally, she'd have had plenty of time for work, but the storm of the century had hit Western Washington. It had started with a light dusting of snow on Tuesday night and continued throughout the next day. After finally getting Kaya back to sleep after a night terror at two AM on Thursday, Libby had looked out the window and groaned at the blizzard conditions highlighted by the streetlights outside. With all of the hills in their area, there was no chance the schools would be in session for the foreseeable future.

Her prediction had been right, and they were now on their second snow day. Playing in the snow had lost its novelty sometime that morning and all four kids had come down with cabin fever. She'd tried setting up board games for the younger kids, but the afternoon had been a series of "I'm bored" and "There's nothing to do." Her preteen, William, had holed up in his room with his video games, but it was probably about time to limit his screen access.

Reluctantly, she closed her laptop and got up from the desk, crossing the living room to the basement door. When she was only a few feet away, it shot open, ricocheting off of the springy doorstop on the wall behind it. From experience, she deftly stepped aside. Sure enough, her three youngest children hurtled forth, seven-year-old Tommy chasing his sisters with a toilet brush.

"Mom! He's trying to get us with the icky potty thing!" Beth shouted as she ran toward Libby and huddled behind her for protection.

Kaya ran past Libby and jumped onto the couch, bouncing on the cushions with all her might. Tommy was close behind her, still waving the brush in the air. As Libby stuck out her hand to catch her younger son, she was struck with the idle thought that maybe it was time to teach Tommy how to clean the bathrooms. Now *that* would be helpful. Until having two little boys, she'd never realized how bad their aim could be. It seemed like she was constantly cleaning around the toilet.

Tommy smacked into her outstretched arm at full speed, and the toilet brush went flying out of his hand. Libby watched in horror as it bounced off the carpet, its bristles still glistening with liquid of unknown provenance.

Behind her, Kaya stopped bouncing. "Uh-oh," she sang in a high voice. "Tommy's in trouble."

"Eww," Beth muttered. "That's so gross."

Tommy looked up at Libby, his eyes wide. "Oops."

She closed her own eyes for a moment, but the chaos remained when she opened them. "Enough!" she shouted. "Everyone outside. Now." She herded them toward the sliding glass door off the kitchen, where they'd left their damp snow gear earlier that day.

As they were getting dressed in their snow pants, winter jackets, boots, and mittens, Libby ran up the stairs to the second floor and knocked on William's closed door. "William? It's Mom."

"Come in."

She entered to find him sitting at his computer, attention glued to a video game. His eyes flickered to her for a second, but then returned to the game.

"William," she said. He didn't answer, and she moved closer to him, rested her hand on his shoulder, and spoke in a louder voice, "William."

He sighed loudly and continued tapping his index finger on the left mouse button. "What?"

"Can you please go outside with your brother and sisters?" Libby surveyed his room. He'd built up a collection of candy wrappers, soda cans, and dirty plates on his desk. "And where did you get all that candy anyway?"

He shrugged. "Lucas's birthday party last weekend."

"Seriously?" She picked up some dirty clothes off of the floor and dropped them in the hamper. "His parents just sent you home with a ton of candy?"

"Yeah. They're pretty cool." He continued playing his game.

She gritted her teeth, trying to keep her own cool. "Can you please help with your siblings?"

"Do I have to?" he griped. "I'm in the middle of something."

"Yeah, tell me about it," she said, thinking about the catering bid she owed the Rasmussens. At this rate, she'd be done in a week and they'd have already selected another company for the job.

"Can't you do it?"

Pressure rose in her chest and her head pounded. "William! Now!"

"But my game," he whined. "I'm not at a save point."

"I don't care." She was oddly proud of managing to keep a level tone of voice. "Your father's not here to help, so we all have to pull together. Your brother and sisters are driving me crazy."

"That's not my problem." He finally took his gaze off the screen and stared at her defiantly.

Downstairs, the other kids were screaming at each other again. Libby had had enough. Not for the first time, she wondered what it would be like to have a whole apartment to herself like Gabe had in Boise. It must be nice to have a quiet place to work and relax. But, that wasn't in the cards for her right now.

"Enough!" The word erupted out of her mouth like it had been shot from a cannon. She gritted her teeth and pointed her finger at William. "No more backtalk. I need you to help out with the little kids so I can get *my* work done. Okay?"

He glared at her but said nothing.

She took a deep breath and exhaled slowly. "I'm going back downstairs to figure out why it sounds like someone is being murdered in the kitchen. I expect you to be down there in the next few minutes. Understood?"

William stared out the window but gave her a slight nod. Libby took that as an affirmative and left his room.

Back in the kitchen, Beth and Tommy were wrestling on the floor, arguing over which one of them had lost one of their identical black gloves. Kaya was shoving a hat over her stuffed bunny's flat ears and reaching for the sliding glass door.

"Little Bunny is not going outside," Libby shouted at Kaya.

Kaya pouted and lifted the bunny up to show her mom. "But she's all ready for playing in the snow."

Libby groaned. "I don't think bunnies like snow very much."

Kaya opened her mouth as if to argue the point, but Libby grabbed the toy from her and carefully set it down in a kitchen chair that faced the back yard. "Look. Now she can watch you guys."

Kaya narrowed her eyes but didn't try to retrieve her stuffie.

Libby eyed Beth and Tommy, who had briefly stopped actively fighting, but were now sticking out their tongues at each other. She separated them and found the lost glove hiding under the edge of the blue cotton bath towel she'd laid across the floor in front of the door to catch any melted snow.

"Here." Libby slid the glove she'd just located over Beth's bare hand and gave Tommy the one they'd been fighting over. "Put it on and go outside. You guys have way too much energy to be stuck inside all day. William will be out soon to play with you too."

"Fine, but I'm not playing with Tommy." Beth reached past Kaya and opened the door. Both of the girls slipped outside, and Tommy stuck his tongue out at them.

"Tommy," Libby warned.

He sighed. "I know, I know." He stuck his hands in his

jacket pocket and followed his sisters into the fenced backyard.

With the kids' voices muffled by the sliding glass door, the kitchen was blissfully quiet. Libby took the opportunity to refill her coffee cup and carried it back to her desk, then returned to the catering contract she'd been working on earlier. A few minutes later, just as she'd requested, she heard William come downstairs and exit into the back yard as well.

Two hours later, Libby sighed with relief as she finished her email and hit *send*. There was always more work to do, but that had been the only pressing matter for the day—everything else could wait until tomorrow.

She felt bad that she'd been ignoring the kids, because all of them were going a little stir crazy, cooped up in the house. But they'd known she had to work and, judging by the laughter she heard outside, they'd recovered from their argument earlier in the day. Now, though, she hoped to make it up to them. She turned on the oven and pulled a batch of homemade chocolate chip cookie dough out of the freezer.

While the oven was preheating, she unloaded the dishwasher, then put the balls of dough on a cookie sheet and stuck them in the oven to bake when it was ready. In the meantime, she poured milk, cream, sugar, and cocoa powder into a pot on the stove. Her mother had always made hot chocolate on snow days, and Libby had continued the tradition with her own family.

Fifteen minutes later, with hot, gooey cookies on a plate, Libby opened the door to the back yard and shouted, "Who wants hot cocoa and cookies?"

The kids all shouted, "Me!" and ran toward the door. Tommy, Kaya, and Beth piled inside, dripping snow onto the towel. Libby laughed at them trying to disrobe with their thick gloves and coats on, then started helping them.

Tommy was already at the table, halfway through his first cookie, when Libby realized William hadn't come inside yet.

"Where's William? Is he working on his snow fort again?" She peered out the window, but it was getting darker, and the yard was filled with shadows.

Tommy shrugged and stuffed another cookie in his mouth.

"Didn't he go to Brandon's house?" Beth asked, her mouth ringed with a chocolate mustache.

Libby froze as though she'd been hit by an errant snowball. "He was supposed to be playing with you outside."

Kaya's eyes were as wide as the saucer in front of her. "He came out, but then left through the side gate."

"He left? When?"

Tommy shrugged. "I don't know. Right after we went outside, I think." He grabbed another cookie from the plate, completely unaware of the panic rising in Libby's chest.

She tried to convince herself not to panic. William was twelve years old and capable of being out on his own. Usually. Right now, though, the sun was setting, and it was freezing outside. *He's at Brandon's house,* she told herself. *Stop worrying.*

She picked her phone up from her desk and scrolled through her contacts until she found Brandon's mother.

"Hey," she said when his mother answered. "This is William's mom. Is William still at your house?"

"Hi, Libby." The woman sounded surprised to hear from her. "I haven't seen him in a week or two. Maybe he's at Danny's house? I think a few of the kids were going over there today, but Brandon had some schoolwork to catch up on."

"Oh, okay. Thanks for letting me know. I'll check with Danny's parents."

She called them next, but they hadn't seen William either. After she'd exhausted her list of his friends and classmates, none of which had seen him, her panic level rose exponentially.

She returned to the kitchen, where the kids were still having their snack. "Did William actually say anything to you about where he was going?"

Tommy shrugged. "I don't think so?" He grinned. "But I was building up a stockpile of snowballs to throw at Beth, so I might not have heard him if he did."

Libby sighed and looked at the girls. "Did he say anything to either of you?"

"Nope," Beth said. "I thought you'd told him he could go to a friend's house."

"I didn't," Libby said in a tight voice. She fought to tamp down her fears. "If he's not with a friend, do any of you know where he might be?"

"Uh…" Kaya said, holding Little Bunny in her arms. "I don't know where he is, but he was wearing his backpack. Maybe he was going to school?" She glanced up at Libby hopefully.

"Maybe." Libby smiled and kissed the top of her youngest daughter's head, not wanting to worry her.

If William wasn't with his friends, where was he? Had he doubled back and come inside the house without her hearing? She ran through the house, checking every room. Just as Kaya had said, his backpack was missing, as was his Nintendo Switch.

She went back into the living room, out of sight of the kids, and paced the thick cream-colored carpeting. How had she let this happen? She was responsible for the kids, and she'd thought they were safe in the back yard. Gabe had made sure the fence was tall enough that no one could climb over it, and it couldn't be unlocked from the front yard—only from the back, for safety reasons. The kids played out there on the swing set every day, and they'd never had any reason for concern, especially when they were all out there together.

This was different though. William had left their house on purpose. Should she call Gabe and let him know William was missing? No, it seemed a little premature to worry him. Should she call her mom? Her parents lived only a few blocks away and William walked past their house on his way home from school. But he didn't usually go there just to hang out, and she didn't want to admit to her mom that she had no idea where her son had disappeared to. She'd just told Debbie that she had everything under control while Gabe was gone and that she didn't need any special help.

Her stomach churned, and fear won out over her embarrassment. She dialed the familiar number. "Mom?"

"Libby," Debbie answered. Then, in a sharper tone, "What's wrong?"

Libby gripped her phone tighter. Leave it to her mother to always know when her daughters were in distress. "William's gone."

"Gone?" Debbie echoed. "What do you mean gone?"

"I mean he left the house and I can't find him. He's not with any of his friends either." Libby bit her lip to keep from crying. She'd always prided herself on staying calm in a crisis, but the stress of being a single parent for the last month had brought all of her emotions to the surface.

"Okay." Debbie paused, then continued. "I'm sure he's

fine. He's a smart kid and he knows not to stay outside in the freezing cold."

"Do you think he'd come over to your house?" Libby asked.

"Maybe?" Debbie replied. "I'll check the back yard." Libby heard her mother walking across their hardwood floors and the sound of a door sliding open. "Whew. It's cold out here," Debbie said.

"I know." Libby couldn't help thinking about how William's arms were starting to poke out of the sleeves of his winter coat. He'd gone through a growth spurt recently and she'd meant to take him shopping for a new one, but hadn't done so yet. If he hadn't found shelter, would he be warm enough? Should she call the police to help search for him?

"Honey," Debbie cut into Libby's spiraling thoughts. "He's here. In the playhouse."

Libby let out the breath she'd been holding, and her eyes filled with tears. "He is?"

Debbie's voice was warm. "He's here, and he's fine." Muffled voices sounded in the background, and then Debbie was back on the line. "I'm going to bring him inside with me."

"Can I talk to him?" Libby asked, suddenly consumed with a desire to make sure he was actually okay, a ridiculous concern because her mother had just told her he was fine.

Debbie hesitated. "I don't think he's ready to talk to you just yet. Maybe give him a bit of time to calm down?"

"I'm coming over now." Libby hung up and shouted to the other kids. "Get your jackets on. We have to go get William from Grandma's house."

"Grandma's house?" Beth asked. "Why's he there?"

"I want to go to Grandma's house," Kaya said. "Little Bunny loves tea parties with Grandma."

Libby couldn't help smiling, even though she didn't know how to feel otherwise. "Little Bunny can come with, but I don't think there will be any tea parties today. But make sure you don't drop her." She shuddered. Having to deal with a beloved stuffed animal soggy with snow or mud today might send her over the edge of sanity.

"Okay," Kaya sang out.

They all got their winter gear on, traipsed through the back yard, and exited out to the brightly-lit sidewalks that the city had kept clear. Their area had received at least a foot of snow, and if Libby hadn't been so distracted, she would have loved to have gone for a peaceful walk outside. She'd always loved how quiet the world seemed when blanketed in a thick layer of snow. Now, though, her every thought was focused on getting to William.

14

Debbie

As Debbie slipped the phone back in her pocket, she imagined Libby getting the kids ready to go, barking orders at them with the efficiency of a drill sergeant. Without a doubt, Libby would have her kids marching along the sidewalk to Debbie's house within minutes. Debbie turned her attention back to William, who was sitting on the love seat in the playhouse, no longer playing on the Nintendo Switch he'd received for Christmas, and wearing an expression of defeat.

"Mom's coming here, isn't she?"

Debbie offered him a small smile. "I'm afraid so, kiddo." She looked around the room, rubbing her hands on her sleeves to ward off the chill in the air. Although the playhouse was equipped with electricity, William hadn't turned the heater on, and the only jacket Debbie wore was the sweatshirt she'd slipped on as she left the house. "It's freezing out here. What do you think about moving inside?"

He nodded and carefully put the game system back into its case, tucking it into the main zippered compartment of his backpack. Debbie stood on the flagstone path just outside the small cottage door while she waited for him to join her. Her husband, Peter, had built the playhouse back when their own girls were young, and kids had loved playing in the structure ever since. Now she was grateful that William had thought of seeking shelter there.

They walked back to the house together and she got him settled at the table with a blueberry scone while she made both of them some tea. By the time the kettle whistled, all that remained of his scone was a pile of pale crumbs.

"William," she said, "how long were you out there?" She poured hot water over the blueberry herbal-tea bags he liked, releasing a sweet fragrance into the air.

He shrugged, then looked at the watch on his left wrist. "I don't know. Maybe an hour or two?"

"Why didn't you just knock on the door to our house? You know you're always welcome here." She set two cups of tea on the table and sat down in the chair next to him. "Your mom was in quite a panic when she realized you were missing."

He jutted out his chin. "I didn't want her to know where I was." He sighed and looked into the steaming cup of tea in front of him. "I guess that didn't work out so well."

This wasn't like William. He'd always been the typical eldest child, obedient and responsible, just like his mother.

She tilted her head and scanned his face. "What's wrong, sweetie? Did you and your mom have a fight?"

He sighed and stared longingly at the plate of scones she'd placed in the center of the table. Debbie pushed the platter closer to him and he eagerly reached for it, grabbing another scone and scarfing it down as though he hadn't eaten in days.

Finally, he wiped the crumbs away from his mouth with the back of his hand and said, "My mom won't let me do what *I* want to do. Since my dad left, she always wants me to help with the little kids. She doesn't really care about me at all." He looked down at the empty plate, his eyes glistening with unshed tears.

Debbie's heart twisted. Her eldest grandson was obviously in more distress than any of them had realized. "Oh, sweetie, I'm sure that's not true. Your mom loves you very much." She took a sip of tea and eyed him thoughtfully. "I think with your dad gone, things have been a little harder for her than she'd like to admit."

A tear rolled down his cheek and dampened the shoulder of his royal-blue Minecraft T-shirt. "I miss my dad so much. He used to do things with me, like play basketball or video games." He hung his head and muttered, "Mom doesn't have any time for me."

Debbie leaned forward and squeezed him tight. He melted against her chest like he had as a small child, his tears now falling freely down his cheeks. "I'm so sorry, sweetie. Your mom is doing her best, but she's got a lot on her plate."

He sniffled loudly and she gently released him. Reaching behind her, she grabbed a tissue from the box on the counter and handed it to William.

He blew his nose with a loud honking sound and said earnestly, "I know she misses my dad too. I've been trying to help, Grandma. Honest, I have. I shoveled off our front walkway yesterday and I helped Beth and Tommy with their homework earlier this week." His voice took on a hint of bitterness. "But the rest of my friends all get to play video games or do whatever they want on snow days. Mom always wants me to help with my brother and sisters so she can work." He stuck out his lower lip. "It's not fair."

Debbie shook her head and smiled wryly at him. "I'm sorry to inform you, kiddo, but life's not always fair. Your mom didn't want your dad to go to Idaho any more than you did." It was a life lesson that everyone had to learn, but it was hard to make a twelve-year-old boy understand. "Family sticks together. When someone in our family is in need, we all have to chip in and take care of them, or pick up the slack when they're not able to do something."

She thought she'd been trying to do that with Libby, but now she wondered if her efforts had backfired and caused Libby to become even more fiercely independent.

William drank some of his lukewarm tea. He sniffled, then met her gaze. "I just want things to go back to the way they were."

She rubbed his back in slow, comforting circles. "I know, sweetie. I know."

The doorbell rang then, and Debbie could hear William's siblings talking loudly on the front porch.

William looked up at her. "Is that Mom?"

She nodded. "I'm afraid so."

"Do you think she'd let me stay here for a little bit longer? He stared down at his empty plate, then peeked up at her. "I mean, if that's okay with you, Grandma."

Debbie smiled and pushed herself up from the chair. "I'll see what I can do." She walked through the short hallway to the front door and opened it. Sure enough, Libby and her other kids were standing on the porch.

Libby pushed past her, having already taken off her wet snow boots. Her eyes were wild with fear and a hint of anger. "Where's William? I can't believe he ran off like that."

Debbie held the door open wider to allow the children in. They made a beeline for the basement where she kept all of their toys and games. She closed the door and gestured to the kitchen. "William's in there." Before Libby could take off in that direction, Debbie caught her arm and said, "Go easy on him. He's having a hard time with his dad gone."

Libby gritted her teeth. "I know he is. We're all having a hard time with Gabe gone. But that doesn't mean he can just run off like this." Her voice trembled. "I was worried sick about him."

Debbie smiled and patted Libby's arm. "I seem to remember a certain little girl doing the same thing when she was about William's age. Do you remember when you and Meg ran off and hid in an alley down the street?" Debbie shivered, still remembering how terrified she'd been when she realized her daughters had disappeared. "I had no idea where the two of you were."

Libby blushed. "That was different."

Debbie raised an eyebrow. "Really? How so?"

Libby sputtered. "It just was. You and Dad had threatened to ground Meg and I over something—I don't even remember what it was now. We just wanted to get away from everyone for a little bit."

Debbie peered at her eldest daughter and said slowly, "Okay, but what do you think William is doing?"

Libby's face crumpled and drained of all color. As if in a daze, she walked over to the sofa in the living room and plopped onto its soft cushions. She buried her head in her hands for a moment, then gazed up at Debbie.

"Having Gabe gone is so much harder than I thought it would be," she admitted. "I didn't realize how much he does around the house or how much we'd all miss him."

Debbie sat down next to Libby on the couch and

pulled her eldest daughter close. Libby melted into her just like William had done earlier.

"I don't know what to do, Mom." Her words were muffled against Debbie's chest.

Debbie rocked her gently and whispered, "It's going to be okay, honey. It's going to be okay."

She'd hoped to reassure Libby, but, instead, her daughter only cried harder. From the other side of the room a flicker of movement caught Debbie's attention. William stood in the doorway, his eyes wide as he watched his mother bawling like a small child in her mother's arms. Debbie shook her head slightly in an attempt to get William to leave before he alerted Libby to his presence. His mother didn't need to know he'd seen her crying. William opened his mouth, about to speak, but he took his grandmother's hint and quietly padded off in the opposite direction.

Libby stopped crying long enough to grab a wad of Kleenex from a box on the end table and furiously swipe at her face. "I don't know what's gotten into me, Mom." She hiccupped loudly. "I really didn't think this would be so hard."

"I know, honey. Is there anything I can do to help?" Debbie handed her a fresh handful of Kleenex.

Libby gave her a sad smile as she accepted the tissues. "I don't even know. I thought I could do it on my own, but obviously I can't. My kids hate me. I can't get all of my own work done for the business. I just feel like I'm failing at everything in my life."

Debbie couldn't help but laugh. She shook her head ruefully. "Oh, honey. That's just how it is to be a mother. You're always juggling too many plates and sometimes a few fall off the stack."

As if sensing his mother had finished her crying jag,

William reappeared in the doorway. Debbie motioned for him to come over to the couch and she slid away from Libby to make room for him. Libby looked up as William sat down between them.

"Mom." William peered at Libby with an anxious expression.

She didn't say anything, but reached out and pulled him close to her in a tight hug that made William yelp. "I'm sorry, baby."

Normally William would have protested the term of endearment but this time, he just let her hug him. "I'm sorry too, Mom." He pressed his lips together and then said, "I can help out more with the little kids. I don't mind, honest." He grinned. "Well, most of the time."

She smiled at him through watery eyes. "You already do a lot, and I appreciate all of it, even if it sometimes doesn't seem like it."

It sounded like they were well on their way to mending their relationship, so Debbie quietly stood up and tiptoed away to give the two of them their privacy. Her cell phone rang from where she left it on the kitchen counter, and she quickened her pace to get there before it stopped ringing.

"Hello?" she answered.

"Hi, Debbie. It's Zoe."

"Oh, hey, Zoe." Debbie was always happy to hear from her daughters' good friend, who also happened to be the lead event planner for the Inn at Willa Bay, where Debbie was having the cancer fundraiser in a few weeks. "How's everything going? Is Shawn enjoying his sister's visit?"

"He is," Zoe answered. "Jessa is really nice, and I'm glad I've had a chance to get to know her a little better. When I still hadn't met her after nearly a year of dating

Shawn, I almost started to think she was a figment of his imagination."

Her voice held a touch of hesitancy, as though she wasn't telling Debbie everything about Jessa's visit. Debbie didn't know Zoe well enough to pry though, so she didn't question her like she would have her own daughters.

Zoe paused for a moment, and Debbie wondered if the call had dropped. Sometimes cell service could be finicky in parts of Willa Bay. "Zoe, are you still there?

Zoe sighed. "Yeah, I'm still here." She cleared her throat. "Actually, I was calling because I have some bad news."

Debbie's heart thudded in her chest as she immediately began thinking the worst. Her middle daughter lived on the resort property. Had something happened to her? "What's wrong? Is Meg okay?"

"Oh! Meg's just fine," Zoe said quickly. "Sorry, I didn't mean to worry you about that."

"Oh good." Debbie sighed with relief, which quickly turned into a sense of foreboding. If Meg was okay, it had to be something to do with the fundraiser. "What is it, then?"

Zoe took a deep breath and then the words spilled out of her mouth. "It's the tents that we had reserved for your event. With all the snow we've had in the area, the event rental company had a problem with their roof caving in. They think it happened sometime last night, but it wasn't discovered until this morning."

"So, what exactly does that mean?" Debbie asked as she paced the vinyl kitchen floor.

"Unfortunately, the part of the roof that caved in was over their storage area." Zoe paused again, obviously hating to give bad news. "I'm so sorry, but the tents you reserved were damaged."

"Okay," Debbie said slowly. "Are they going to be able to get me something else for the event?"

"I don't know. They just called me about an hour ago and they're still trying to assess the full extent of the damage. It doesn't sound hopeful though. I get the feeling that a large portion of their inventory was affected by the collapse." Zoe exhaled loudly. "I've been wracking my brains to figure out a solution. There aren't any other local companies that carry tents of that size, but I might be able to find something out of the local area."

"Oh." Debbie sat down at the kitchen table and picked up the now-cold cup of tea. She swirled the dark red liquid, sending a berry-scented aroma through the air as her mind raced furiously. Despite being scheduled for February, her fundraiser was going to take place outdoors, when the chance of precipitation ruining an outdoor event was high. What was she going to do without the large, heated event tents? It was too late to find another venue, and Zoe had given her a great deal on the Inn at Willa Bay. Besides that, having it at a different venue wasn't in the budget, even if there was an availability elsewhere.

Zoe's voice came over the line again, this time a little brighter and more confident. "I'm sure we'll figure something out, Debbie. It's going to be okay. I've never had an event go completely sideways and I don't intend to let it happen to yours. I just wanted to keep you updated about what was going on."

Debbie picked up the empty scone plates and teacups from the table and brought them over to the sink. "Thank you for calling. Let me know if you figure something out, and I'll try to do the same on my end."

"Sure thing," Zoe said. "And try not to worry. I promise you it will all work out. I'll talk to you later."

"Thanks."

The phone went silent, and Debbie set it down next to the sink. She rinsed the dishes and loaded them into the dishwasher, but her mind wasn't on the task. What was she going to do if they couldn't locate replacement tents?

A rumbling sound like a herd of thundering elephants came from the basement stairs, and her younger grandchildren burst into the kitchen. "We're starving!" They cried out. "Do you have anything for us to eat?"

Debbie grinned. There was nothing like a bunch of hungry kids to distract her from her troubles. She glanced at the clock on the wall over the side window. It was getting close to five. "Let me ask your mom if it's okay. I don't want to ruin your dinner."

Debbie went back into the living room where Libby and William were chatting about Minecraft. They were both smiling as they talked, so it seemed as though they'd patched up their differences.

"Hey, Libby?" Debbie said. "Do you want me to give the other kids a snack?"

Libby checked her watch and made a face. "No. I need to get dinner started. I'll give them something small as soon as we get home." She stood from the couch and stretched her arms out in front of her. "Is it okay if William stays over for a few more hours? I think he could use a little more time away from his siblings."

Debbie smiled. "Of course. He's welcome to stay for dinner or as long as he'd like."

William's face brightened at the idea of time away from his brother and sisters. Libby called out to the rest of her kids to get ready to go. As they put on their coats, they mumbled loudly about how hungry they were.

She rolled her eyes at Debbie. "They act like they

didn't just have cookies before we left. Even lunch was only a few hours ago."

Debbie gazed at her grandchildren, who were now dressed in a colorful array of cold-weather jackets. She recognized Kaya's pink parka as one that Beth had worn a few years prior. "They're growing boys and girls."

"Yeah, and eating me out of house and home," Libby grumbled, but she wore a smile on her face. She herded them out the door, where they took a few minutes to put on their boots on the front porch.

Debbie waved goodbye to them as they traipsed off down the sidewalk. When they were out of sight, she closed the door and said to William, "Do you want to help me with dinner? I've got a few things you can choose from."

William nodded. "Do you think we could have Swedish meatballs? I love them, but mom never wants to make them."

Debbie mentally reviewed the contents of her refrigerator and freezer, then rested her hand against his back. "Yep, I think we can do that. I've got some frozen meatballs in the garage."

"Awesome," William cried out as he ran toward the kitchen.

Debbie followed a few steps behind him. Worries about the fundraiser loomed over her, but at least she'd been able to help fix things between Libby and William. As she'd told Libby a while earlier, being a mom was like having a bunch of saucers in the air. This time, even though her fundraiser plate was spinning just out of reach and threatening to crash to the ground, she'd managed to restore peace in her family. For today, one out of two wasn't bad.

15

Andrew

Andrew's computer emitted a swishing sound, and he looked up from the document he was reviewing to glance at the screen. He hoped the e-mail he'd just received was from Sam, because he still hadn't heard back from her about the job offer. Though it had not yet been a week since he'd talked to her about the position, he became increasingly concerned as time went on that he should have let Headmaster Weatherbee know he'd offered the permanent position to Sam. He knew his boss wouldn't care that he'd made the offer on his own, as it was well within his rights and responsibilities as assistant head-master to make hiring decisions, but he still liked to run things by his boss first.

A quick scan of his email showed that it was from one of the other teachers at the school, not Sam. He checked the time in the corner of his computer screen—almost four o'clock. The headmaster didn't usually leave for the day until close to five, so he should still be able to catch him. Andrew rolled his chair back from his desk and went down the hallway to the headmaster's office. He rapped lightly on the closed door.

"Come in," Arthur said.

Andrew turned the doorknob and entered the room. His boss's office was nearly twice as big as Andrew's and outfitted with a large executive-style desk, leather office chair, several tall bookshelves, and a coffee table in front of a black leather sofa. Arthur Weatherbee stood next to his desk, placing several manila file folders into a dark-brown briefcase.

"Oh," Andrew said with surprise. "I've caught you at a bad time."

"No, no," Arthur said. "It's fine. What can I do for you? I'm about to head out, but I've got time for a quick question."

Andrew shifted on his feet. "This might take longer than you have today. I wanted to talk to you about hiring for the housemother and P.E. teacher role for next year, as well as a few other things about the budget. It's not urgent though."

Headmaster Weatherbee frowned and checked his watch. "Hmm. It sounds like we might have a bit to talk about. I'm supposed to meet Dan Rigby at the club in half an hour to play racquetball." His face brightened as though a lightbulb had turned on. "Hey, why don't you come over for dinner tonight—maybe around seven-thirty? We can chat for a few minutes before dinner and then you can try out my wife's new cooking obsession. She's been taking Indian cooking classes down at the community center, but with the kids gone, she hasn't quite mastered cooking only enough for the two of us." He scrunched up his face. "I've been eating curry for half of my meals for the last two weeks. It'd be great for somebody else to share in the wealth."

Andrew chuckled as an image popped into his head of Tupperware containers filled with endless varieties of curry. "I do love Indian food. If your wife is really okay with it, I'd be happy to come to dinner tonight."

"Oh, thank you," Arthur said with relief. "You're a lifesaver." He ruefully eyed his slightly paunchy midsection. "Or, rather, a stomach-saver, in this case. I think I've gained five pounds in the last two weeks."

"I'm happy to help. I hope you enjoy your racquetball game, and I'll see you later." Andrew walked back to his own office, deep in thought.

Though it would have been great to get this matter off of his chest right away, he couldn't fault Headmaster Weatherbee for meeting with one of the school's biggest donors. After all, Bayside Prep's scholarship fund was largely made up of alumni donations. Since Andrew had been the beneficiary of one of the scholarships as a high school student, he was grateful for the fundraising efforts that would help even more students attend his school.

He sat down in his own office chair, marveling at how different his space was than the headmaster's. It wasn't the size of the office, necessarily—it was more the overall atmosphere, which he'd hoped to emulate. Both Arthur's and Andrew's offices were filled with books and similar dark furnishings, but it struck Andrew just now that the biggest difference lay in all of the little touches that made the headmaster's office more homey.

While his boss had photos of his wife and his two college-aged girls on display, Andrew didn't have any personal mementos. Arthur had a picture of Skamish Bay on his wall that a former student had painted for him, and he took great pride in the gift. Andrew surveyed his mostly blank walls, as if seeing them for the first time. The only decor was a painting of a clipper ship at sea, left behind by the former occupant of this office. He concluded that his space was long overdue for a makeover and some personalization.

He glanced over at his computer screen, noting that five more emails had appeared in the brief time he'd spent down the hall. Reluctantly, he pulled himself away from his mental redecoration plans and got back to work.

At seven-fifteen, he left his office and drove the few blocks around the campus perimeter to the headmaster's house. He pulled into a small three-car alcove on the side of the circular driveway and got out of his car. It had been only a little over a month ago that he'd been there for the New Year's Eve party, but he still took the time to admire the grand manor house, which never failed to impress him.

What would it be like to live there? *Maybe someday*, he thought. While he didn't openly profess his aspirations, he secretly hoped to be considered for the headmaster's position when the older man retired.

He jogged up the front steps and rang the doorbell.

Arthur's wife, Linda, opened the door. "Hi, Andrew. We're so happy you were able to come to dinner tonight."

"I hope it's not an imposition," he said as moved past her and into the high-ceilinged entry hall.

She shook her head vigorously. "Oh no. Definitely not an imposition. Arthur always says I make enough food for a small army." She held out her hand and gestured to an open doorway midway down a long hall. "He's waiting for you in his office."

Andrew paused before heading in the direction she'd indicated and breathed in the tantalizing aroma of chicken and spices that filled the air. "Something smells wonderful."

She beamed at him. "I made chicken tikka masala and fresh naan. I'm sure Arthur told you all about the cooking classes I'm taking. I think I'm starting to get the hang of Indian food, but I guess you'll have to be the judge of that."

He smiled back at her. "I'm looking forward to trying it." He looked down the hall. "So that's his office? The first door on the left?"

"Yep. You can go right in." A timer dinged from somewhere across the house and she perked up. "Ah. I think my naan is done."

She scurried off toward the kitchen, and Andrew slowly walked toward Arthur's office. In all his years of working at Bayside Prep, Andrew had never been invited over to the headmaster's mansion for dinner. As he neared the office, he felt as though he were about to enter his boss's private domain. He knocked lightly on the open door and Arthur looked up.

"Andrew, good to see you. Pull up a chair." He motioned to a small wooden armchair positioned against the wall.

Andrew obliged, dragging the chair until it was situated across the desk from his boss. "Thanks for meeting with me."

Arthur laughed. "You don't need to be so formal. It's no problem." He stroked his salt and pepper beard. "In fact, I don't know why Linda and I haven't had you over for dinner more often. We'll have to remedy that in the future."

Andrew let his gaze wander around the room. The furnishings were similar to the headmaster's office on campus, but he'd managed to add even more personal touches to his home office. Heavy blue drapes framed a square window behind the desk, their formality softened by sheer, floral-patterned curtains behind them. A bulletin board on the wall opposite the window held drawings done by a child's hand and a plethora of what appeared to be family vacation photos. As Arthur's daughters were well past the crayon age, Andrew assumed these held sentimental value.

"So, what did you want to talk with me about?" The headmaster's question pulled Andrew back to the present.

Andrew pulled some files out of his briefcase. "I wanted to give you the latest budget numbers." He pointed at a line he'd highlighted in yellow. "It looks like we should have enough money by the beginning of next year for the addition to the gymnasium."

Arthur raised his eyebrows in surprise. "Really? By next September?"

Andrew nodded. "We've had quite a few large alumni donations, in addition to some successful fundraisers."

"That's wonderful." Arthur tapped his finger against his bearded chin. "Now we'll be able to increase the number of opportunities on our sports teams. I always felt bad that we weren't able to have a JV team for some of the sports, due to lack of space."

Andrew slid the file back into his briefcase and set it on the carpeted floor. "On that note, I wanted to talk to you about the P.E. and housemother position."

His boss cocked his head to the side. "Oh, did Pila decide not to come back next year?"

Andrew shook his head. "Her husband is being transferred to a duty station somewhere on the East Coast. With a new baby, she obviously wants to go with him."

Arthur leaned back in his chair and tented his fingers

in front of him. "Well, I'm sad to hear she's leaving, but at least we have plenty of time to hire someone for the role."

Andrew moved to the edge of his chair. "Actually, that's the other thing that I wanted to talk with you about." He glanced down at his hands in his lap and then back up to Arthur. "I offered Samantha Briggs the position."

"Oh?" The headmaster leaned forward. "Is she interested in continuing on for next year?"

"I don't know. She said she'd think about it." A rush of hope shot through him, and his words seemed to bubble out before he could censor them. "I really hope she does say yes though. The kids love her, and she's really passionate about what she does. There's even talk that our girls' basketball team may go to State this year."

The headmaster's lips quivered as though he were trying to smother a grin. "You seem to have a very high opinion of her."

Heat crept up Andrew's neck from under the collar of his shirt. "She came to Bayside Prep with several years of experience teaching physical education, and she relates well to all of her students."

"And that's all?" Arthur's eyes seemed to drill into him.

Andrew resisted the urge to squirm in his seat like he was a child being reprimanded by the school principal. "She's just a great teacher and an asset for our school."

"Uh-huh." A wide grin spread across the headmaster's face. "And do you know your eyes light up when you talk about her?"

Andrew froze. He thought he'd done a pretty good job at keeping his budding feelings for Sam close to his chest. He attempted to feign innocence, hoping he'd misunderstood. "I'm sorry, sir?"

"Is there something going on between the two of you?" Arthur held up his hands. "No judgment if there is."

Andrew shook his head vigorously. "No, of course not. I'm indirectly her supervisor, and I know that type of relationship wouldn't be appropriate."

The headmaster studied him carefully. "You know, if you did have feelings for her, it would be okay." He continued, "We don't have any hard and fast rules about relationships between campus personnel. If the two of you want to pursue something, it's okay by me."

Now, Andrew did squirm. "Sam—" he stopped and corrected himself, "*Ms. Briggs* is a wonderful teacher." He sighed. "And, truth be told, if it were under different circumstances, I'd consider pursuing something with her. But it's not."

Arthur removed his glasses, wiping them with a soft cloth he removed from a drawer in his desk. "Listen. I know we don't usually talk about such matters, but hear me out. Life is short, and sometimes you just need to take some chances." He looked at the picture of his wife on his desk. "Did I ever tell you that Linda and I met on campus?"

Andrew cocked his head to the side. "Really?"

Arthur smiled. "She was a history teacher when I first started as headmaster. Like you, I tried to resist her charms, but eventually I gave in, and we started dating." His expression softened as he gazed fondly at the photo. "And that was it."

"I didn't know." Andrew was so surprised by this revelation that he couldn't think of anything else to say. This was the most intimate conversation he'd ever had with his boss, and he wasn't sure how he felt about the new development in their relationship.

Arthur chuckled and put the microfiber cloth back in

the top drawer. "It's not something I talk about a lot. But it's not something I'm ashamed of either. All I ask of my staff is that you maintain professionalism on campus. What you do in your personal life is none of my business." Something behind Andrew caught his attention. "And speak of the devil."

Andrew turned to see Linda Weatherbee in the doorway.

"So I'm the devil now?" She shot her husband a mock glare. "Anyway, dinner's ready." She smiled at them, spun around and disappeared down the hall.

Arthur watched her leave, then regarded Andrew thoughtfully. "Was that everything you wanted to go over?"

Andrew nodded. "Everything and more."

The headmaster got up from his desk and clapped Andrew on the back. "Sorry to get personal. It's just that I see you working so hard, and in the whole time I've known you, I've never heard you talk about dating anyone seriously." He eyed Andrew. "Or, rather, I don't really hear you talk about your personal life in general."

"Probably because I don't have much of a personal life." Andrew gave him a lopsided smile, but Arthur's words hit him hard. He'd pushed aside any personal relationships in the last few years in favor of excelling at work. "I'll give some thought to what we talked about."

"Good." Arthur cleared his throat and moved toward the door, gesturing for Andrew to follow him. "I'm glad we had this talk. Now, let's go try some of Linda's tikka masala."

Andrew followed Arthur down the hall until they reached a dining room with a long mahogany table surrounded by Duncan Phyfe chairs. Three place settings were positioned at the far end, and in the center, Linda had arranged tureens of rice, a mixed-vegetable medley, and a still-bubbling dish of a creamy reddish-orange sauce covering bite-sized chunks of meat. A platter nearby was piled high with a variety of seasoned naan, including one that looked like the garlic kind from Andrew's favorite Indian restaurant.

Andrew's stomach grumbled at the aromas of garlic, cumin, coriander, and ginger. "This looks and smells amazing," he said to Linda. Arthur sat down at the head of the table and Andrew took one of the chairs next to him.

"Thank you." Linda's face lit up with pleasure, and she sat down across from Andrew.

They dug into the feast. When he could eat no more, Andrew wiped his mouth and leaned back in his chair. "That was delicious—every bit as good as any Indian restaurant I've been to in the area."

Linda glowed with his praise. "Oh, I don't know about that. But it was good, wasn't it?" A small smile glimmered on her lips.

Andrew eyed the half-full serving bowl of tikka masala in front of him. He wanted more, but he knew it would be too much. He said to Linda, "You can invite me for dinner anytime you want. Living by myself, I don't take the time for many home-cooked meals."

"Arthur and I will definitely have to do that. We've enjoyed your company tonight." She reached over and patted her husband's hand. "I know Arthur is a little tired of eating my concoctions."

He smiled back at her. "Oh, I don't know about that, sweetie. You know I love your cooking."

Her eyes lit up. "Hey, speaking of cooking, do you think that the Culinary Club students would like to learn this recipe? I've been trying to figure out what to make next week."

Arthur nodded. "I bet the students would love this."

"Perfect!" She turned to address Andrew. "Do you cook?"

He smirked. "Does popping a TV dinner into the microwave count as cooking?" Her eyes widened in response, and he laughed. "That's what I normally have for dinner. I actually do enjoy cooking, but I don't have many opportunities to cook for anyone other than myself, and it hardly seems worth the effort for just me."

Linda pointed her index finger in the air. "I have a great idea. You should help me with the Culinary Club. I bet the students would love having you in the kitchen—it would let them see an entirely different side of you."

"Oh, I don't know about that," he demurred. "I'm definitely not a professional chef."

"Oh, me neither." She swiped her left hand through the air as if brushing away his concerns. "But as long as the kids are having fun and learning some useful life skills, it doesn't really matter." She peered at him. "So, what do you think? Do you want to help lead the cooking demonstration next week?"

Every bone in Andrew's body was shouting at him to say no. To his surprise, though, the opposite response popped out of his mouth.

The headmaster's eyes bounced between them like he was watching a tennis match. "Well, honey, sounds like you found your new co-leader."

She rubbed her hands together in glee. "Ooh, we can cover so many things with the two of us teaching."

Her husband's lips quivered with a barely repressed smile. He looked at Andrew pointedly. "Maybe you'd like to hone your cooking skills by inviting a certain someone over for dinner at your place?"

This time Andrew couldn't stop the heat from rising into his cheeks.

Linda eyed Andrew. "Are you seeing someone?"

Andrew shook his head. "No, not really."

The headmaster interjected, "But he's thinking about it."

"Well, I'm sure she'd enjoy having him cook her a meal, but a man can never go wrong with dinner at a nice restaurant either. In fact, I just heard about a lovely steakhouse over on Tanger Street." She seemed to realize Andrew's love life might be a sensitive subject for him, and she glared at her husband. "But let's leave that up to him, okay?"

Andrew shot her a grateful smile as she stood and cleared the table. Arthur asked if she needed help, but she insisted she was fine, so he invited Andrew into his office for an after-dinner drink. Andrew stayed for another two hours and greatly enjoyed the chocolate lava cake à la mode that Linda had prepared for dessert.

By the time he left, he was so stuffed that he feared he'd need to roll himself out to his car. Despite his concern over the dinner invitation, the evening had gone much better than he'd expected. The headmaster and his wife had been wonderful company, and Andrew found himself wanting to spend more time with them.

Was this what his life had been missing? He'd been focused on work for all these years, but it had come at the cost of personal relationships. That was something he definitely needed to remedy.

The next day, Andrew found Sam sitting at her desk in her small office off of the gymnasium after all of the students and the other P.E. teachers had left for the day. The door was open, but he cleared his throat to alert her to his presence.

Her eyes registered surprise when she saw him. "Hi. Did we have a meeting scheduled?"

He shook his head. "No. I was just in the gym checking on something and I thought I'd stop in to say hi." He stuffed his hands in his jacket pockets and looked around her office.

"Oh." She fidgeted with a pencil on her desk. "Hi, then."

His stomach churned uncomfortably, and he wondered if he was making a mistake. It had been ages since he'd had romantic feelings for someone, and he found himself at a loss for words. Her expression became more and more concerned as the silence loomed between them. "Are you okay? Is there something else you needed to talk to me about?"

"Yes, sorry." He cleared his throat again and forced himself to meet her gaze. It shouldn't be this difficult to ask someone out. "I was wondering if you might want to join me for dinner some night."

She cocked her head to the side. "You mean like a date?"

His heart hammered in his chest, but he nodded in the affirmative.

She fiddled with the pen again, then pushed it away and looked up at him. "I'd like that."

"Oh." He'd half expected her to turn him down.

She laughed, reminding him of how much fun they'd had together in the park. "You did invite me on a date, right?"

"Yes." He blinked a few times. "I did. I was thinking maybe tomorrow night at six?" Should he invite her over to his house for dinner? What if she thought he was a horrible cook? Or didn't like his apartment? He shook his head. This was way too much pressure for a first date.

"Linda Weatherbee told me about a wonderful new steak-house in town. Does that sound okay to you?"

"It sounds great."

"Okay, then." He managed a weak smile. "I'll see you tomorrow night."

"See you then."

He turned around and walked out the door, not knowing how he should feel. Part of him was excited about the date, but another part of him was terrified. He was glad he hadn't invited her to his apartment though. If things went well on their date, he hoped there would be plenty more occasions to impress her with his fledgling culinary skills.

16

Sam

"I think you should wear the red sweater with those black dress pants." Mandy held up a soft cashmere sweater Sam had received for Christmas and turned her gaze to the pile of footwear Sam had flung onto the floor from the small clothes closet. She tapped her finger against her lips and looked thoughtful. "You should wear those black leather ankle boots."

Sam nodded, grateful for one less decision to make. She'd been staring at her meager wardrobe for at least ten minutes, unable to choose an outfit to wear on her date with Andrew.

Mandy checked her watch. "I'd better get going or I'll be late for my own date. Have fun, and don't do anything I wouldn't do." She gave Sam a quick hug and a wink before hurrying out of the room.

Sam slipped off the leggings and long tunic she'd worn during the day and stepped into the black dress pants. She pulled the ruby-red cashmere sweater over her head, then examined her reflection in the full-length mirror on the closet door.

Not bad, she thought. Her brown hair skimmed her shoulders in soft waves, and the mascara she'd swiped on earlier made her brown eyes pop. The soft fabric of the sweater caressed her skin in a comforting manner.

Although butterflies danced in her stomach whenever she thought about her date with Andrew, they were in fierce competition with the thoughts about her future swirling around her head like a funnel cloud. What did she want to do? In the last six months, her world had been turned upside down, and for the first time she could remember, she didn't have a clear vision for the rest of her life. Owning the dance studio could be an amazing opportunity—something she'd never even considered before. But was it right for her at this point in her life? Would a ballet studio be profitable enough to support her? She didn't need much, but she did have a certain fondness for eating and having a roof over her head.

And, she couldn't discount the job Andrew had offered her. While all of her previous experience had been with high-school students, she enjoyed coaching the girls' basketball team and teaching elementary P.E. classes at Bayside Prep. Most of all, she'd been surprised by how much she enjoyed her role as housemother for the younger girls.

From its perch on the window ledge, her phone beeped insistently. Sam picked it up to find a flurry of text messages from her mom.

Meg said you want to work with me in the catering company next year.

Is that true?

Call me back.

Oh, and have fun on your date.

Sam groaned. Did everyone in her family know she had a date with Andrew? She'd only told Meg, but she should have known the news would quickly spread through the family grapevine.

The phone chimed again with another text from her mom. Sam tapped the button to call her.

"Hello?" her mother answered breathlessly. "Sam?"

"Hi, Mom." Sam paused for the inevitable barrage of questions.

Her mom didn't disappoint. "So, who's this guy you're going out with? Have you been dating for very long? Has anyone in the family met him yet?" Her voice held a tinge of excitement.

"Mom!" Sam sighed. "It's our first date. It's not like we're getting married next week, or anything. And no, no one has met him yet." She looked out the window at the darkening sky over the campus. "You'll be the first to know when we get engaged." She laughed at the thought. It had barely been five months since she'd ended her engagement with Brant.

"Well, I'd better be!" Her mother laughed too. "Sorry, honey, it's just that it's been a while, and I was worried you weren't going to get out there again after how things ended with Brant."

"I know." Sam had shared her mother's concerns. Even now, she wasn't sure she was ready to date again, especially considering the potential land mines that could accompany dating someone she worked with. Her stomach twisted and she started to regret accepting Andrew's invitation.

Her mother seemed to sense Sam's hesitancy and deftly changed the subject. "So, what's this I hear about you wanting to join the family catering business next year? I was a little surprised when Meg mentioned you were interested, but with Libby moving away, I could really use the help."

Sam stared blankly out the window now, not registering the shadowy rows of trees in front of her. She hadn't given much thought to working with her mom, but Debbie obviously had.

"Sam?" her mom nudged. "Are you still there?"

"I'm still here." Sam slumped into the comfortable armchair she'd brought with her to Bayside Prep. "I was just thinking about the catering job."

"I'd love to have you," her mother said. "You've always been a big help in the past."

"I do like catering," Sam conceded. "Let me think about it a little more, okay?"

"Sure. Of course," her mom assured her, then quickly added, "No pressure. I know you've got a lot on your plate right now."

"Thanks, Mom." Sam leaned back in the chair and closed her eyes for a few seconds. Even though her family could be a pain, they were always there for her. Now, though, she had even *more* options for her future, and she wasn't sure she liked that.

"Well, I'll let you go now," Debbie said. "I'm sure you need to get ready for your date."

"Thanks. I hope you and Dad have a nice weekend. I love you."

"Love you too, honey. Have fun on your date." Debbie hung up and Sam set the phone down beside her on the chair.

Thirty minutes later, Sam walked across campus to the far parking lot where she'd agreed to meet Andrew. The secrecy felt weird, but neither of them wanted the students to know they were going on a date. As housemother, she was held to a high standard, and she'd prefer not to entertain questions from her students about going out with the assistant headmaster.

She made her way to the end of the lot where he'd said he'd meet her. He was leaning against the side of his sedan, nervously tapping his fingers against his leg. A tenuous smile spread across his face when he saw her. He walked around to the passenger-side door and opened it. "You look very nice." He paused and his smile faltered. "It's okay to say that, right?"

She chuckled. He was every bit the school administrator, hyper-aware of the rules for romantic interactions in the modern world. "Yes, and thank you." Apparently, Mandy had made a good choice with the outfit. She slid onto the seat, and he shut the door, then walked around to the driver's side. When he took his seat next to her, she was suddenly aware of how close they were in such a confined space.

Before they left the parking lot, he turned to her. "Is dinner at the steakhouse still okay? I made a reservation for tonight." He tripped on his words a bit, as though he were just as nervous as she.

"Sounds good to me." She settled into the soft cloth seats as they drove away from campus.

"Um, have you been to many restaurants in Paddle Creek?" he asked politely, his eyes focused on the road.

"A few." She swallowed a lump in her throat. The last time she'd eaten out at a nice restaurant with anyone other than one of her sisters or a friend had been with Brant. Truthfully, she much preferred a good hamburger joint to a fancy steakhouse, but Andrew seemed enthusiastic about the place they were going.

Next to her, Andrew pressed his head into the headrest and tightened his grip on the steering wheel. She stared out the window as they passed through the center of town. Conversation with Andrew had come easily when they'd met up by chance and eaten lunch together. Why did things feel so awkward now?

She turned to him. "Does this feel weird to you?"

His eyes widened, but he kept his attention focused on the road. "Is something wrong?"

"No, no." She bit her lip. "I think it's just been a while since I went out with someone new. My last relationship was pretty long-term."

He nodded. "I'm no expert at dating either." He turned into a large parking lot in front of a newer-looking building. "This is it." They both removed their seatbelts, but neither made any effort to get out of the car. Suddenly, he blurted out, "Would you rather go somewhere else? Maybe somewhere fun like Jack & Carney's?"

Did she want to go to a casual restaurant attached to a huge arcade? *Yes, please!* She reached for her seatbelt and snapped it into place. "I'd love that." She sighed. "To tell you the truth, I wasn't too excited about the steakhouse."

He raised an eyebrow. "Why didn't you say so before? We could have made plans to go somewhere else."

She shrugged. "You seemed like you wanted to go there."

He laughed and started the car again. "I only mentioned it because Linda Weatherbee swore you'd like it." He wrinkled his nose. "I'm more of a BBQ guy, myself."

"Oh, thank goodness." His admission lifted some of the pressure from their date and reignited her desire to have dinner with him.

Five minutes later, they parked in front of the neon-yellow sign for Jack & Carney's Roadhouse. As they walked in, tantalizing aromas of grilled hamburgers and spit-roasted meat made Sam's stomach growl. She'd been nervous before their date and hadn't been able to eat much all day. Now, she couldn't wait to order.

In front of them, games of all sorts filled a massive, gymnasium-sized room. Lights flashed on the machines and cheers erupted from a group of people bouncing along on a mat in front of the Just Dance game. After they'd waited for only a few minutes, the hostess led them to a table in a corner of the restaurant away from the arcade games and handed them menus.

"Have you been here before?" Andrew asked.

"Nope." Sam surveyed the menu, pleased to see a full page dedicated to gourmet hamburgers. "But I've been wanting to try it. My oldest nephew raves about their food, and, of course, all of the games to play after dinner."

"I came here once for my niece's birthday party, and I can assure you that you won't be disappointed." He finished looking at the menu and set it on the table. He peered at her. "This is better, isn't it?"

"A whole lot better." She made her selection and set her menu on top of his. "I think I was letting the pressure of a first date and everything else in my life get to me. This was just what I needed."

When the waitress came over, they placed their orders, then sipped on the strawberry lemonades she brought back for them.

Sam glanced across the restaurant to the brightly lit arcade space. "So, what's your game of choice?"

He surveyed what they could see of the games. "I've always liked Skee-Ball. How about you?"

She didn't hesitate. "The one where you shoot baskets."

"I guess that makes sense, since you're a basketball coach." He set his lemonade on a paper coaster. "Have you always played?"

"Since I was a kid, but not seriously until my junior year of high school. Before that, I was pretty obsessed with ballet." She traced her pointer finger through the condensation on the side of her glass. "What about you? Do you play any sports?" She snickered. "Besides Skee-Ball, I mean."

He shot her a mock glare. "I happen to be a Skee-Ball champion, thank you very much. But if you must know, I actually played baseball in high school and college."

"Oh, wow." With his sweater vests and glasses, Sam hadn't pegged him as an athlete. Then again, people were often surprised to find she'd once considered a career in ballet. "I had no idea."

"I've been playing since I was a kid in Little League. Unlike academics, it was something I was good at."

"Your parents must have been really proud of you," Sam observed.

He shrugged. "Eh. My dad went to my games when I was younger, but after I got a needs-based scholarship to Bayside Prep and really got serious about playing, it was like he didn't care anymore."

"Oh, I'm sure that's not true." Sam scanned Andrew's face. His playful attitude had disappeared when he'd mentioned his father. "Bayside Prep is quite a distance from where your family lives, right?"

"About an hour. But that wasn't it. He drove long distances for work all the time. He could have come to see me play." He took a long gulp from his lemonade. "I think he was disappointed that I left home and didn't want to follow in his footsteps with the farm."

"Hmm." Sam played with the wrapper from her straw. She'd struck a sore spot with Andrew. She didn't want to let it ruin their date, but she sensed his relationship with his father was something that really bothered him, and she hoped he'd share more about it.

"Anyway," he continued. "I had to stop playing my junior year of college because I tore my rotator cuff. Although disappointing, it was probably the best thing to ever happen to me, because I threw myself into my studies and realized how much I wanted to go into school administration." He stopped talking and smiled at her. "Enough about me though. What made you decide to go into teaching?"

Their food arrived before she could answer. They spent the next twenty minutes scarfing down the delicious burgers, laughing at each other when various sauces spilled out of the sandwiches and onto their plates. When they'd finished mopping their faces with the wet wipes the waitress provided, they paid the bill and walked over to the arcade, where they loaded money onto a game card.

"So, what should we do first?" Andrew asked.

Sam pointed at the Skee-Ball lanes and grinned at him. "I think I need to see a champion in action."

"Your wish is my command." He took her arm and guided her over to an empty machine. After tapping their game card on the payment device, he grabbed a ball and rolled it down the lane with surprising speed. It neared the top, then ricocheted off the side and landed neatly in the corner pocket.

"Okay, maybe you weren't lying to me about your Skee-Ball prowess." They played a few games, but she didn't score nearly as high as him. "My turn." She took his hand and pulled him over to the basketball-toss game.

"Let's see what you've got." He stood aside to give her more room.

Knowing he was standing next to her made her

nervous and she missed a few easy throws, but she still managed to get a decent score.

"Nice." Andrew nodded approvingly. He held up a basketball. "This has never been my sport. Care to give me a few pointers?"

She laughed and moved in closer to him. "First, hold the ball like this." She moved his hands into place and then steered him around to face the hoop. "And then just bend your knees and throw it."

He made a face and tossed the ball. It bounced off the rim and rattled down into the guts of the machine. "I could use some more practice."

"Maybe just a little." She tried to keep a straight face but failed miserably. It felt like she'd stepped into one of those romantic comedies where the guy uses golfing lessons as an excuse to hold a girl close, except this time she was the instructor. "Okay, let's try again."

This time, the ball went straight through the net with a satisfying *swoosh*. Andrew's eyes lit up and Sam grinned. They may have been on a date, but seeing someone achieve a new skill reminded her of why she loved teaching so much.

He whooped loudly and gave her a quick hug, then backed away, his eyes wide. "Sorry, I didn't mean to..."

"I didn't mind." She put her hand on his arm and let it linger for a bit longer than necessary. Her heart beat faster as their eyes met.

A smile slid across his lips, brightening his whole face. "I'm having a really good time with you tonight."

"Me too." A warm glow spread throughout her body. "I think I really needed a night out like this." She sighed. "I've been so stressed about everything, and it's been nice to just let loose a little—especially with good company."

"I'm glad you're enjoying yourself." He nodded at a

photo booth a few feet away and held out his hand. "What do you think? Should we commemorate this evening?"

"I'd love to." She took his hand, and he led her over to the photo booth. Once they were sitting on the bench inside of it, he slipped his arm around her and she leaned against him, her smile genuinely happy as the camera flashed.

17

Jessa

It was oh-dark-thirty when Shawn pulled up to the cottages they'd assigned to Jessa after finding out she was staying awhile. He'd borrowed Zoe's sedan to take Jessa to the military hospital in Tacoma for her surgery, because it got better gas mileage than his full-size Chevy truck. The small car threw off a snaking cloud of exhaust in the frigid, early morning air as he ran up to meet her on the porch.

Jessa didn't bother objecting when her brother grabbed her small suitcase and wheeled it down the ramp toward the car. In a matter of hours, she'd be undergoing major surgery, and this wasn't the time to assert her independence. She followed slowly behind him, holding on to the railing to maintain her equilibrium.

She got into the car, fastened her seatbelt, then turned to Shawn, who'd done the same. "Thanks for taking me today."

He flashed her a smile, but even in the dim light, she

could see it didn't quite reach his eyes. "No problem. That's what brothers are for."

"I could have stayed at Dad's house." She kept her gaze trained on Shawn.

"You could have. But I figured you'd rather have some privacy the night before your surgery." He started down the long driveway, the headlights illuminating the gravel road and the tall trees on either side of it.

He was right. As much as she loved her dad, she'd enjoyed sleeping in the comfortable bed in her cottage that she'd grown used to over the last week. That, and she'd avoided any unwanted conversations about her surgery. It may have been inevitable, but she hadn't wanted to dwell on it.

They drove in silence until they'd reached the freeway and were headed south to Tacoma.

"Traffic's light," Shawn said idly.

"Good." She'd hoped if they left early enough, they'd be through Seattle before the early morning rush hour. Her plan seemed to be working so far, as they were moving smoothly along the four-lane freeway.

"Um." Shawn stared straight ahead, but she could tell he wanted to say something.

She sighed. "Spit it out."

"Jessa." He swallowed hard. "I'm worried about you."

She looked down at her lap, where she'd been twisting the ends of her jacket between her forefingers and thumbs, then turned her attention to her older brother. "I'm going to be fine. The doctor said it's a fairly routine surgery—I mean, as far as brain surgeries go." She touched his arm gently when he sucked in an uneasy breath. "Don't worry." She pasted a bright smile on her lips, even though she wasn't sure he could see it while driving. "I'm not worried at all."

He nodded. "This is hard for me. I want to protect you, like I've always done."

"Some things I have to do on my own." She laughed. "Besides, where were you when I was deployed to Iraq? I can handle myself."

His gaze flitted to her for a split second before refocusing on the road ahead. "I know, but I still hate that there's nothing I can do to help."

"You are helping." She shifted slightly in her seat to face him. "You're taking me to the hospital. And you're picking me up when I'm ready to go home, right?"

Her voice had held a teasing tone, and he responded in kind. "I don't know... Maybe I'll just leave you there for a while." He grinned when she slugged him lightly on the shoulder. "Oh fine." More seriously, he said, "You know I'll be there as soon as you wake up."

"I know." If there was one thing she could count on, it was her family. She'd spent much of her life away from them, but when she'd been diagnosed with a brain tumor, her first thought after processing the news was that she wished she lived closer to them. She settled back in her seat and looked out the window.

Seattle's skyscrapers towered over them, surrounding the freeway on either side. Office windows glittered like glow-in-the-dark checkerboards, waiting for their occupants to arrive for the day. While she couldn't see Elliott Bay in the dark, the Space Needle was decked out in golden lights, looking much like what its designers had envisioned for their 1962 World's Fair building of the future.

She leaned closer to the window to get a better view as they zoomed past. "I missed this."

"The city?" Shawn asked. "I didn't think you spent much time up here when you lived in Washington.

She shrugged. "I didn't. But there's something about this area that feels like home. When I was stationed in landlocked posts like Fort Leonard Wood in Missouri, I always felt like something was missing."

He nodded slowly. "I get it. That's why I stayed in South Carolina after I got out of the Army. It was close enough to the water to remind me of home."

She laughed. "And then, of course, you ended up back here anyway."

"That I did." Shawn quieted as he changed lanes to ensure they wouldn't accidentally take the airport exit.

"Was it weird for you to find out about Celia?" She still had trouble thinking about the elderly woman as her grandmother and it didn't come naturally to refer to her as such.

"Yeah, definitely." He shook his head. "When Zoe called me up to tell me that a woman named Celia was in the hospital and had left my name as her emergency contact, I thought she'd made a huge mistake." He glanced over at Jessa. "But I'm glad it wasn't." His voice softened. "If it hadn't been for Grandma's accident, I'd probably never have met her—or Zoe."

Jessa changed the subject. "Do you think you and Zoe will get married?" They passed under a streetlight, allowing her to see his face had flushed. She peered closer at him. "You've thought about it, haven't you?"

"I've got a ring for her in my dresser drawer," he admitted. "But I'm not sure when to pop the question."

"Oh, wow." She sat back. "You really have been thinking about it."

With her impending brain surgery, construction on the cottages of the Inn at Willa Bay, and the everyday chaos of living on the grounds of an event venue, she and Shawn hadn't had as much time to talk as she would have liked. Shawn had recently turned forty, and she was fast approaching the "Big Four-Oh" herself. Both of them had been so devoted to their Army careers that marriage had always seemed like a far-off prospect. Now, though, he was making the leap toward a new future with Zoe.

"So, what do you think?" His voice trembled uncharacteristically, and his fingers tightened on the steering wheel.

"About marriage, or life in general?" she teased.

He rolled his eyes. "No, doofus. Me marrying Zoe. You like her, right?"

Jessa thought back to meeting Zoe when she'd first arrived in Willa Bay, almost a month ago now. Her brother had introduced his girlfriend with so much pride in his voice, and Jessa had been impressed with the way Zoe looked at him. Since then, Zoe had become someone Jessa was happy to call a friend. "Yeah. She's okay."

"Just 'okay'?" He stared at her in alarm and the car swerved slightly. "Do you not like her?"

"Hey! Keep your eyes on the road! I'd rather not die on my way to the hospital."

"Oh. Sorry." He faced forward. "But really—do you like her?"

"I was messing with you." She patted his arm. "Zoe's great and I'm thrilled for both of you, honest."

Seeing her brother so happy did make her wonder about her own future. She'd planned to stay in the Army for another ten years, but the brain tumor's appearance had pretty much forced an early retirement. Although she had her twenty years in and would be receiving a full pension, she couldn't see herself retiring from all work at age thirty-eight. But what was she going to do for a career? Where was she going to live?

She shook her head to clear it. She still had a brain

surgery and post-op recovery to get through before she could even entertain thoughts about the future.

"You okay?" Shawn asked.

"Yep." She looked out the window, surprised to see the miles had flown by. "We're almost to the base, aren't we?"

"Just a few more miles. We already passed the exit to Dad's house."

"Wow." Her stomach twitched. At the start of the almost two-hour drive, she'd been able to avoid thinking about her surgery. Now, it was quickly becoming a reality that she'd go under the knife in a matter of hours.

By the time he pulled the car up to the Army hospital's entrance, her insides were at full spin, and she fought to breathe evenly. Still, when she got out of the car to take her rolling suitcase from Shawn, she thought she did a pretty good job of pulling off an air of confidence.

"Do you want me to go in with you?" He shifted his weight from foot to foot, as though he wasn't sure what to do.

"Nope." She leaned over and gave him a hug. "I'll be fine. I'm sure there's plenty of paperwork to fill out. Besides, I've got some trash TV to watch on my phone while I wait. How else am I going to catch up on what the Real Housewives of New Jersey are up to?"

His eyes darted to the sliding doors of the hospital behind them. "I don't know. I feel like I should go in with you."

"I'm fine, really." She grabbed the handle and prepared to start rolling it toward the doors. He surprised her by reaching out and wrapping his arms around her in a bear hug that threatened to lift her off of her feet. "Hey!"

"Sorry." He reluctantly released her, and she caught sight of tears glistening in his eyes before he swiped his hand over his face. "Must be something here I'm allergic to," he grumbled.

"Probably." She smiled and gave him a quick hug. "I'm going to be fine though. Really."

"I'll be here when you're through with surgery. Dad and I both will."

She wanted to argue that it was unnecessary, but it did make her feel better that they'd be there when she woke up. Although the doctor had said the surgery was relatively routine, it was the first time she'd undergone full anesthesia, and she wasn't sure how she'd feel afterward.

"See you later, alligator." She gave him a wave and swiveled her bag around to get a better grip on it.

"In a while, crocodile," he said, automatically finishing the phrase they'd uttered many times as children.

She heard him get back into the car and she faced the hospital, walked forward, and let the giant sliding doors swallow her.

Two hours later, she was in the pre-op room, trying not to let anxiety take hold of her. She'd already undressed and donned the scratchy cotton gown they'd given her, so she unpacked the headphones she'd stashed in the side pocket of her carry-on and connected them to her phone. Flipping through the media, she selected the playlist she'd compiled, which was heavy on calming Frank Sinatra tunes. Just hearing him croon always brought her back to her childhood, and the memory of her parents dancing cheek-to-cheek in the living room.

A tear trickled down her own cheek at the thought of her mother. She'd been taken from them way too soon, and Jessa still missed her after all these years. Now that Celia had come back into their lives, Jessa caught glimpses of her mother in her grandmother's face and mannerisms, even though the two of them had been separated soon after Celia gave birth.

Jessa took a deep breath and changed the song to something with fewer memories attached to it. She planned to go into surgery with a positive mindset, not with worries swirling around in her brain. With that thought in mind, she closed her eyes and visualized waking up in the recovery room with the doctor standing over her, telling her that the surgery had been wildly successful.

"Jessa?" A woman's voice cut through her meditation.

Jessa's eyes snapped open, and fear clawed at her insides. So much for the happy thoughts she'd been curating. "Yes," she managed to stammer.

The nurse smiled at her and took a few steps closer to the whiteboard on the wall that listed Jessa's name and pertinent information. When she moved over to the bed, the thighs of her pink scrubs made a scratching noise as they rubbed together. "I'm Nancy. I'm going to be getting you ready for surgery today."

Jessa nodded and tried to regain her composure. Soon, she'd be in the recovery room, just as she'd imagined.

Many hours later, Jessa woke to a sore throat and a grogginess that she couldn't seem to shake. She forced her eyes open and scanned the small, curtained room. Somewhere outside of her little nest, people were talking about their weekend plans, sending an irrational surge of anger through her. It wasn't fair that she was laying there with bandages wrapped around her head and they were discussing their upcoming trip to the ocean.

A machine behind her beeped and was quickly

followed by a hand parting the thin curtain that offered little privacy from the rest of the recovering surgery patients. A woman's friendly face poked around the curtain. She seemed familiar, but Jessa couldn't remember her name. She tried to smile at the woman, but failed miserably.

"Oh good, you're awake. How are you doing? You probably don't remember me, but I'm Nancy. I was with you in the pre-op room." The nurse rested her hand on the side of the bed and peered at Jessa. "Are you thirsty?"

Jessa tried to nod, but the effort made her head spin. Her mouth felt like the Sahara Desert, and her throat burned from the breathing tube.

Nancy seemed to understand, because she held up a damp sponge to Jessa's lips. "I bet your mouth is pretty dry. I'm sorry I can't give you anything to drink yet, but this should help."

That thing is supposed to quench my thirst? Jessa eyed the sponge, but dutifully closed her lips around it. The cool water did little for her throat, but it did moisten her mouth like a magical elixir. "Thanks," she croaked.

"No problem. I'm going to check you out, and then we'll get you moved into your new digs, okay?"

Jessa managed a slight nod, then fell back against the pillow, exhausted. She sensed bulky bandages on the back of her head, but didn't have the energy to reach up and feel for them. At the moment, she wasn't in too much pain, but she knew that would come when the heavy drugs wore off. Her surgeon had warned her she'd be out of it and tired for a few days, but until now, she hadn't quite understood the magnitude of that warning. She tried to stay awake while Nancy took her vitals, but she couldn't fight the siren call of sleep, and soon fell into a whirling vortex.

She woke up in a single hospital room, which was spacious compared to her cubicle in the post-op area. A different nurse stood by her side, checking her vitals yet again and making notes on an electronic chart.

"Hi, Jessa," the new nurse said. "I'm Alice. I'll be taking care of you for a while."

"Okay." It probably wasn't the right response, but it was the only thing Jessa could think of to say. She couldn't hear anyone else in the room besides Alice. Where were Shawn and her dad? "My family?"

"They've been here a while in the waiting room. I'll let them know you're settled in. Do you want to see them?"

"Maybe for a minute." Jessa closed her eyes again. When she opened them, her father, Shawn, and Zoe were standing next to her. "Whoa." It took a lot to focus on all of them, and everything was a little blurred.

"How do you feel?" Her normally stoic father's voice caught on his words.

"Like a truck ran me over." She sighed, even that tiny movement causing waves of dizziness to cloud her thoughts.

"Maybe we'd better leave Jessa alone for a while," Zoe whispered to Shawn. "I think she could use her rest."

Thank you, Zoe. She'd never liked her potential sister-in-law more than she did at that moment. Jessa appreciated that her family had come to see her, but the surgery had been more demanding than she'd expected, and she really just wanted to sleep for the next few days.

Her father cleared his throat. "Honey? Would you prefer for us to go home for a while?"

"I'm so tired," she whispered in response.

Shawn laid a warm, reassuring hand on Jessa's arm. "We'll come back tomorrow morning, okay?"

She gave him a meek smile, and they tiptoed out of the

room. Once again, she was alone, but found she was having trouble going to sleep. The nurse had left the lights on low and the machines in Jessa's room and down the hall beeped incessantly. *Why can't they just let me sleep? How is anyone supposed to rest in a hospital?*

Her annoyance built, and she tried to remember some of the positive affirmations she'd been working on. None came to her. All she could remember was the old adage, "This, too, shall pass." It was true—in a matter of days, she'd be out of the hospital and working toward recovery in her own little cottage at the Inn at Willa Bay. That thought gave her comfort, and she finally drifted off to sleep.

18

Andrew

Andrew parked his car next to his sister's minivan and mom's old sedan, right in front of his parents' farmhouse. Thankfully, his dad's beat up Ford truck was nowhere to be seen. Although he knew his father would be there for Liv's birthday dinner, at least Andrew wouldn't have to endure a round of inane small talk with him before dinner.

He reached over to the passenger seat and picked up his present for his sister. Liv collected a line of fairy figurines and had been looking for one of the rarer fairies for years, so he'd been keeping an eye out for it on eBay. He'd pretty much given up hope of ever locating it, and then one finally popped up in January, which he claimed immediately. He walked up the steps to the house, knocked on the door, and stepped back.

His niece, Kinsey, flung the door open. "Uncle Andrew!" She wrapped her arms around him, barely avoiding knocking the gift out of his arms. She took a step back and eyed the brightly wrapped box. "Is that for Mom?"

"It is. Do you want to take it to her?" He held it out to Kinsey. She nodded and he handed it to her, then followed her inside, closing the door behind them.

Kinsey veered left toward the living room, but Andrew could hear the older women chatting in the kitchen. The familiar aroma of tomatoes and Italian spices wafted down the hallway, growing stronger as he neared the kitchen at the back of the house. When he entered the large, bright kitchen, his mom was at the stove, stirring a pot of marinara sauce with a scarred wooden spoon. Liv sat at the vintage vinyl-topped table, forming golf ball sized meatballs with her hands.

"Some things never change," he said as he entered the room. "It's always spaghetti and meatballs for Liv's birthday dinner."

Liv looked up and smiled. "Why would I want something else? Mom makes the best spaghetti in the world."

Tammy Hodgins set the wooden spoon on a ceramic spoon rest Andrew had given her many Christmases ago. He came over to her and gave her a hug.

"It's good to see you," she said.

"You too." He hugged her a little tighter and looked around the room. "Do you need any help with dinner?"

"I could use some help with the meatballs," Liv interjected. "You and that kid of mine will eat a ton, and I want to make sure there's enough for all of us."

He eyed the two muffin tins she'd already filled with one meatball in each well. Judging by the scent of roasting meat in the air, there was already a batch or two in the oven. "Sure. Although it looks like you've already got enough for an army." Andrew washed his hands and dried them on a flowered hand towel hanging from one of the drawers. He sat down across from Liv at the table and reached for a portion of the ground meat mixture.

She frowned at him. "What are those, mini meatballs?" She plucked a handful of meat from the bowl and showed him the correct portion size.

Andrew grinned. He'd long ago grown used to his younger sister's bossiness. He added more to the meatball he'd formed and placed it in the muffin tin in front of him. Outside, a truck's engine rumbled to a stop, followed by the thud of its door being slammed shut. His father was home.

"So, what's new?" Liv asked. "Any new girlfriends I should know about?" Her eyes widened as his cheeks warmed at her teasing words. "There is someone," Liv hissed. "Mom was right!"

Andrew's gaze shot over to the stove, where his mom stood over the pot of simmering marinara sauce. Although she faced away from them, he could tell by her stiff posture that she was only pretending to not be eavesdropping on their conversation.

He sighed and stared up at the ceiling before meeting his sister's intense gaze. "Okay, okay. I'm seeing someone." He started rolling another ball of meat between his palms.

His mom dropped all pretense of cooking and pulled a third chair up to the table. "Who is she? You didn't mention her before."

"That's because it's relatively new." He brought the full tray in front of him over to the counter near the oven. "We've only been out on one date." He flashed back to the day he and Sam had eaten lunch together the day of the snowstorm. "Well, maybe two."

"But you like her?" his mother prodded. "How did you meet?"

"She's actually a teacher at Bayside Prep," he admitted.

He leaned against the counter, glad to put some room between himself and the grilling he was receiving from the female members of his family.

Liv laughed. "Ooooh, that figures. I wondered how you'd ever meet anyone. That place is your life."

Tammy swatted Liv on the shoulder. "Enough." She then gave her daughter a pointed look. "It's not like you get out much either."

"Hey, I have a full-time job and a daughter to take care of. I don't have time for anything else." Liv looked at her messy hands and grimaced, then went over to the sink to wash up.

Andrew swallowed hard. Liv's life couldn't be easy.

"So?" His mother said eagerly. "What's she like?"

Thinking of Sam made him smile. "Sam's great. She teaches P.E. and is a housemother for the younger girls' dorm. She took over for one of our teachers who went out on maternity leave."

"Is she from around here?" his mother asked. "What's her family like? Does she like kids?"

He held up a hand. "Whoa. We've only gone out twice together—and one of those wasn't even a real date." His mother shrugged and he knew she wasn't going to give up easily. He chuckled and gave in. "She's from Willa Bay and is very close to her family there. And I'm going to assume she likes kids, or she wouldn't be a teacher." He thought about how hard Sam had fought for Kimmy's happiness, and his heart swelled with a sense of pride so strong it shocked him.

His mother raised an eyebrow. "She sounds like a keeper." She got up and patted his shoulder. "Don't do anything to mess this one up."

He froze. "What do you mean?"

She hesitated, as if searching for words, then said,

"Every time you get close to someone, you push them away."

"I do not." His words were hollow, even to his own ears. She was right. It didn't happen often, but in the past, whenever he grew close to a woman, he found himself finding a reason to end the relationship.

"You do too," Liv confirmed. A timer dinged and she removed three trays of meatballs from the oven, then replaced them with the others that they'd just filled. "Remember Joanna? And Casey? They didn't last long."

"They weren't right for me."

Tammy brought a large pot over to the sink and filled it with water, then set it on the stove. After setting the burner knob to high, she turned to Andrew. "Come with me."

He cocked his head to the side and furrowed his eyebrows. "Why?"

"I want to show you something." She led him out of the room and down the hall to the living room, where Kinsey was flopped out on the couch watching a cartoon on TV that Andrew didn't recognize. His mother stopped in front of a tall oak bookcase and slid a full-size photo album off of the top shelf.

"What is it?" Although his mother loved scrapbooking, Andrew had never seen this particular album before.

Tammy cast a glance at Kinsey, who hadn't budged from the couch, then motioned for him to follow her into the bedroom she shared with his father. She closed the door and handed him the album. "Here. See for yourself."

He opened it up and was instantly hit with a blast of nostalgia. Every page was filled with newspaper articles, photos, and mementos from his days as a high school and college baseball player. He sat down on the bed and looked up at his mother. "I've never seen this before. When did you put all of this together?"

She shook her head. "I didn't."

He let the book close in his lap. "What do you mean? Who made this?"

"Your father," she replied, a glimmer of a smile on her lips.

"What? When?" Andrew didn't know what to think. While his father had pushed him to practice harder than any of the other kids on the baseball team, he hadn't attended many of Andrew's games after Andrew moved away from Barsten.

"I know you don't think so, but he cares about you. He attended every game of yours that he could."

Andrew opened the album again and flipped through the pages. There were photos of him with his teammates, both during and after the games. "I don't understand." Andrew stared at the pages filled with photos of his younger self. "Did he take all of these? I never even knew he was there."

His mother shrugged. "He didn't want to bother you or your friends."

"But why didn't he ever say anything? I always thought he didn't care about me. Except for when I failed, at least."

She cracked a smile. "You may not have noticed, but your father isn't the best communicator."

"That's an understatement," he said with a touch of bitterness.

"Grandma?" Kinsey knocked on the door and opened it a crack to peek in. "Mom says dinner is ready."

Andrew's mother took the album from him and set it on her dresser. "Great! Can you let Grandpa know too? I think he's downstairs."

"Okey-dokey," Kinsey sang out just before she dashed away.

"Look, I'm sure your father had his reasons for not telling you he was at those games or that he's followed your career, but that's something you should probably ask him about, yourself." Tammy moved toward the door and opened it fully. "Now, let's go celebrate your sister's birthday."

Andrew nodded. Her revelation had thrown him for a loop. All these years, he'd thought his father couldn't be bothered with him. It had colored so many parts of Andrew's life and caused him to stay away from home more than he'd have liked. But what if he'd been wrong about his dad?

In a daze, he followed her to the dining room and dutifully took his place where Kinsey instructed him to sit. In front of him, the meatballs he'd helped make were arranged neatly on a platter, accompanied by a giant bowl of spaghetti noodles and marinara sauce. A Caesar salad and a foil-wrapped loaf of garlic bread rounded out the feast. He did his best to participate in the conversation at the table, but he was so wrapped up in his own thoughts that it was hard to follow what everyone else was saying. After dinner, they all helped clear the dishes, then Kinsey had something she wanted to show her mom in the living room and Andrew's dad retired to his office in the basement, leaving Andrew and his mother alone in the kitchen.

"Do you want me to wash the dishes, Mom?" Andrew held up a stack of dirty plates he'd taken from the table.

"No, no. I'm good." She eyed him appraisingly. "You know, this might be a perfect time for you to talk with your dad. He's always in a good mood after a carb-filled meal."

Andrew hesitated, still holding the plates. He'd much rather wash a mound of dishes than have a one-on-one conversation with his father. But, the look on his mother's face told him he didn't have much of a choice in the matter. Reluctantly, he set the plates in the sink.

His mom nodded encouragingly. "Talking with him will help, I promise."

"Fine." He uttered an exaggerated sigh, pressed his lips together and walked toward the stairs to the basement.

His dad had constructed an office in their semi-finished basement back when Andrew was a kid. The main office for his business was located in a small mobile building closer to the fields, so his home office was more of a man cave. By the time Andrew reached the room, his dad had already turned the TV on and was sacked out in his leather recliner chair.

When he saw Andrew standing in the doorway, he sat up and muted the TV. "Did you need something?"

No, this is a mistake. Andrew took a step backward, but his father motioned for him to come in.

"What is it?" Jeff Hodgins pointed the remote at the TV and turned it off completely.

Andrew cleared his throat and shuffled forward a few paces. "Um."

His father cocked his head to the side, as if sensing Andrew had something important to discuss. "Do you want to sit down? I don't have another comfortable seat to offer, but you could take my desk chair if you'd like."

"Uh. Sure." Andrew pulled out the desk chair, but didn't move it out into the room. For some strange reason, having the heavy metal desk between them gave him a measure of confidence. "Dad," he began. "Mom showed me a photo album you compiled."

"Oh?" The older man kicked the recliner's footrest in and sat up straight. "She did?"

"Yeah." Andrew finally met his dad's eyes. "Did you go to my games when I attended Bayside Prep?"

Jeff looked down at his feet, then refocused on Andrew. "I did." He sighed deeply. "I didn't tell you, because I knew how important baseball was to you. By that time, we weren't on good speaking terms, and I didn't want to throw you off your game."

"You wouldn't have." Andrew wasn't completely sure that was the truth, but it would have been reassuring to know his father had cared enough to attend his games. "I would have loved for you to have been there." He wrapped his fingers around the padded arms of the desk chair. "Why did you stop talking to me when I left Barsten? Was it because I didn't want to follow you in the family business?"

"No!" His dad stared at him. "Well, not completely. Of course, I would have loved it if you'd wanted to help me with the farm, but that wasn't the whole reason. I thought you left because you were ashamed of us—our life here. It's not fancy like that school you work at."

Andrew stared at him. "It was never about that." True, he'd wanted to get out of Barsten, but it wasn't because he was ashamed of his family or their livelihood. "Except for baseball, I never felt like I was successful in Barsten. I did so poorly in school because of my dyslexia. When I got to Bayside Prep and they helped me with it, I started excelling in school." He paused, remembering how elated he'd been to get his first A in an English Literature class. "I finally felt like I belonged somewhere. I'm sorry if I made you feel like I didn't want to be here with you and Mom."

Tears glistened in his dad's eyes. "I'm sorry too, son. The school here never mentioned anything about you having dyslexia, so we never even suspected it was a possibility. If we'd known, maybe things would have been different."

Andrew shrugged. "It all turned out okay. If I hadn't gone to Bayside Prep, I probably wouldn't be working there now in a job I love." He offered his dad a small smile. "But I do wish I'd made more of an effort to come home more to see all of you."

"I do too." The older man sniffled and wiped his eyes with the sleeve of his flannel button-down shirt. "But maybe we can work on that for the future. I'd sure like to see your apartment in Paddle Creek, and maybe even the campus where you work."

"I'd like that." Andrew stood and crossed the room. He leaned down and gave his dad a hug. "Thanks for coming to my games. I know it couldn't have been easy for you to make that drive and to take time off from the farm. I really appreciate it."

"You're welcome." Jeff got to his feet and embraced Andrew. "I love you, son."

"I love you too."

After hugging for a few seconds, they broke apart and looked at each other awkwardly.

"It's time for cake," Kinsey shouted from the top of the stairs.

"Saved by cake." His dad clapped him on the shoulder. "What do you think about playing a game of catch with Kinsey afterward? I think she's inherited the family pitching arm." He shook his head and chuckled. "She's beaned me more than a few times when I wasn't quick enough with my glove."

"Sounds like a plan." Andrew grinned at his dad and followed him up to the kitchen.

When he'd come for Liv's birthday dinner, he'd never

expected to make up with his dad after so many years of miscommunications. Now he looked forward to the likelihood that his parents would visit him in Paddle Creek, and maybe he'd even be able to introduce them to Sam. He suddenly had the chance to make up for the lack of personal relationships in his life, and he intended to make the most of it.

19

Sam

Sam raised her right leg to set her foot on the barre. She tested her balance, then hinged at the hips and stretched forward to touch her pink leather ballet shoe. It felt good to move her body, and she was glad she'd decided to practice in one of the empty rooms at the ballet school while Kimmy was in class next door. She continued warming up, lost in her own world, as upbeat classical music drifted through the walls.

The door behind her clicked open and she glanced up to see Tansy walking toward her. "I thought I saw you head in here."

Sam smiled. "I figured I'd get a little practice in while I wait for Kimmy."

Tansy leaned against the barre, looking elegant as always, even in the linen shift and Lycra yoga pants she wore while not teaching classes. "Did you give any thought to what we talked about?"

Sam stopped stretching. She sighed deeply and leaned against the barre as well. "I thought about it a bit." She hung her head. "I'm still not sure it would be a good move for me though. I love being back here, but running a dance studio is so different from what I've been doing."

Sam paused, but Tansy just looked at her thoughtfully without saying anything. The Riverside Dance Studio had been a huge part of Sam's childhood, and she'd only recently come back to it. She didn't want to see it change —or, even worse, go under—if Tansy couldn't find someone to buy the business.

Sam swallowed hard. "I don't know."

Tansy patted her hand. "It's a big decision, and I don't want to rush you." She looked around the room, her eyes misting over as she took in the worn hardwood floors, the full wall of mirrors, and the rectangular bulletin board hanging on the wall near the door. "I'm going to miss this place."

Sam eyed her former teacher. "Are you sure you want to give it up?"

Tansy nodded and managed a small smile. "This studio has always been my passion, but now that my husband is retired, I want to have more time for the next chapter of my life." She bit her lip. "I really wish one of my girls had been interested in taking over though. None of them inherited my love for ballet like I did from my mother and grandmother." She peered at Sam. "Did I ever tell you my grandmother founded the studio?"

Sam shook her head. "No, I don't think so." She knew the studio had been around for decades, but she hadn't realized it had pre-existed Tansy's ownership.

Tansy's eyes sparkled. "Grandma opened it soon after WWII ended, when my mom was in her mid-teens."

"Oh wow. Has it always been in this same location?"

Tansy laughed. "No. She didn't move here until my grandfather retired. Her first dance studio was actually up in Paddle Creek, because he was the headmaster at Bayside Prep."

Sam stared at her. "Are you serious? That's where I'm teaching this year."

"I remember you saying that when you came in last month." Tansy smiled. "Small world, isn't it?"

A thought occurred to Sam. The timing lined up, but it seemed like a huge coincidence. "Was Lucia Davis your grandmother?"

"Yes, why? Have you heard about her?" Tansy asked, her expression puzzled. "I wouldn't have thought her name would still be floating around on campus this many years later."

Sam nodded. "I saw her portrait on a wall with all of the other headmasters. One of the older students put together a biography about her a few years ago and I've been reading it whenever I have time."

"That's amazing." Tansy gripped the barre tightly, as though Sam's words had thrown her off balance. "I'd love to read it sometime."

"Of course. I'll check with the school, but I'm sure they'd have no problem with me loaning it to you." Sam touched Tansy's arm, suddenly noticing her frailty. "Let's go sit down in your office."

Tansy nodded and pushed herself away from the barre. Sam threw on the sweatshirt she'd brought to wear over her leotard, tights and dance skirt, and grabbed her purse from where she'd left it by the end of the barre. They walked together down the short hallway to Tansy's small office.

"Do you want any coffee?" Tansy gestured to the coffee pot on a shelf by the wall. "I made it fresh about an hour ago."

"No, I'm good." Sam smiled. "If I drank caffeine this late in the evening, I'd be up till early morning."

Tansy grabbed a cup off of her desk and filled it. "Not me. I could drink it all night with no problems." She shrugged and walked to the other side of the desk to sit in her chair. "I've always been like that. So..." She paused. "Talk about a blast from the past. I haven't thought about my grandma in a while, but we were quite close when I was growing up. She often spoke about her stint as the interim headmistress of Bayside Prep while her husband was off to war."

"It must have been a lot for her—with her husband gone, she was responsible for the school as well as for her own children." Sam couldn't imagine having such a huge responsibility.

Tansy nodded with a vigor that caused her curls to bob. "It was. Grandma was amazing though. She knew if she hadn't taken on the role as interim headmaster, the school might have closed. She felt like the students already had a lot of change happening in their lives with a war going on, and she didn't want them to have to worry about their school and living situation changing as well."

"Ah." Although Sam had read about Lucia's life, the biography had been rather dry, and Tansy's memories gave her more context for how Lucia must have felt when her husband left.

"She'd been a teacher at the school since before they were married, but by the time my grandfather enlisted in the Army in 1944, they had three kids and a very busy life. Still, she felt it was her duty to take over for him and keep things going for everyone. It was a huge challenge, but she always said she was glad she did it." Tansy looked around her office. "In fact, taking over as headmaster was what gave her the courage to open her own dance studio after her husband returned. If it wasn't for that opportunity, she may never have gone after her dream."

"Wow." Sam fell silent for a few moments. Would she have been able to take on everything Lucia had done? What must it have been like to have all that responsibility in addition to the constant worry for her husband she must have experienced?

Tansy peered at her. "So, what about you? If not the dance studio, what's in the cards for you? Are you going to stay at Bayside Prep? I hear it's a wonderful school."

"It is," Sam agreed. "I do like teaching there." A warmth spread through her, thinking about the students she taught, those that she coached, and the girls who lived in her dorm. The school was growing on her, slowly but surely—as were her feelings for Andrew.

Outside Tansy's office, a door opened and the horde of girls spilled out, crossing the lobby to the changing room.

Sam stood, and motioned to the door. "I'd better go out to wait for Kimmy. I don't want her to worry if I'm not there."

Tansy smiled at her. "Just think about what we talked about, okay?"

"I will." Sam gathered her belongings but stopped in the doorway. "And Tansy—thanks for believing in me after all these years. I know how much the studio means to you, and I'm honored that you would consider entrusting its future to me." She then left the office and walked slowly toward the lobby, her mind racing. Tansy's grandmother had been so brave in taking on a new challenge. Was Sam ready to do the same?

∼

The next afternoon, Sam had a lighter teaching schedule, so she'd made plans to meet her mother for a late lunch at Wedding Belles in Willa Bay. It felt good to get off-campus for lunch, and even better knowing she'd get a chance to talk to her mom. After the last time they'd talked and Debbie had expressed her delight about the possibility of Sam working with her at the catering company when the current school year ended, Sam didn't think that was the option she was leaning toward. Still, it would be good to discuss it more with her.

The café was surprisingly busy at two o'clock on a Friday, but by the time Sam arrived, Debbie had already snagged a table for them.

"Sam! Over here!" Her mother waved at her wildly.

Sam smiled and waved back, then walked over to her. "Good job getting a table by the water."

"I know," Debbie said smugly. "It's always my favorite thing about eating here." The waitress stopped at their table with menus and Debbie smiled at her. "Besides the food and excellent service, I mean."

The woman chuckled and shook her head. "Flattery will get you everywhere, Debbie." She turned her attention to address both of them. "Let me know when you ladies are ready to order."

Debbie had been there so many times that she didn't even bother to pick up the menu. "So, how are things going with you? How did your date go?"

Sam pretended to scan the menu, even though she also knew most of the café's offerings by heart. Should she confide in her mom the concerns she had about dating Andrew? Their date at Jack & Carney's had been great—really great. Sam hadn't had so much fun in months, maybe even years. But what if dating someone she worked with negatively affected her career?

"Sam, are you okay?"

She looked up to see her mom peering at her with a concerned expression on her face. "I'm fine. Just thinking about some things."

"Like what?" Debbie probed. "You've been so tight-lipped lately. I feel like I don't know what's going on in your life anymore."

Sam sighed and looked out the window. "I was thinking about my job at Bayside Prep. I really like working there." She looked directly at her mother. "But I think I like Andrew too."

"Ahhh." Her mother nodded knowingly. "And you're worried about dating someone you work with."

"Yep."

The waitress came over and they placed their lunch orders. She came back immediately with the iced teas they'd both ordered. Sam removed the straw from its wrapper and stuck it in the tall, frosty glass. She took a long drink, savoring the coolness of the beverage.

Debbie pushed her drink to the side and leaned on the table. "What are you concerned about?"

Sam drank more of her tea, then pushed it aside. "If I take the job at Bayside Prep for next year, I'll kind of report to Andrew. He said the headmaster is fine with us dating, but what if things go bad between us? It would be really awkward at work."

Debbie peered at her. "Do you think that would happen—that the two of you wouldn't be able to handle it maturely if you broke up?"

Sam thought about that. Andrew was one of the most professional people she knew, and she couldn't picture him allowing a romantic relationship to affect his work life. "No."

"Then what's the problem?" Debbie asked. "Are you worried about something else?"

"Maybe?" Sam stared out the window again, letting her thoughts drift, like the current of the river flowing in the channel below the restaurant. She took a deep breath and turned to her mom, admitting in a small voice, "When Brant and I broke up, I thought we could still be friends, but look how that turned out. I haven't spoken with him in months." She twisted her napkin between her fingers. "What if that happens with Andrew? I don't want to lose his friendship too."

"Well, what's the alternative?" her mother asked in a matter-of-fact tone. "If you don't date him, you don't risk your job or your friendship with him. But taking the safe path won't allow you to see where things might go between the two of you."

"True." Her mom was right, but it was risky. After the year she'd had, did she have it in her to take that risk?

Her mom smiled softly at her. "Look, life is about taking chances. You have to listen to your heart to reap the biggest rewards. I never thought I'd ever host a huge fundraiser, but it's been an incredibly rewarding experience."

"Were you ever scared to take on such a big project?" Sam couldn't help thinking about Lucia taking on the role of Headmaster at Bayside Prep.

"Of course." Debbie reached across the table to pat Sam's hand. "And I won't say it hasn't been stressful at times, but I think it will all be worthwhile."

Would Sam feel the same way about buying the ballet studio from Tansy? It was a huge risk, and was it even something she really wanted to do? She was finding it more and more difficult to determine if it were fears or a lack of desire causing her to hesitate on decisions about the opportunities she'd been offered. Their food arrived and Sam realized she was hungrier than she'd thought.

"Honey?" Debbie looked up from her food. "It's going to be okay, I promise. When the time is right, you'll know what decisions to make."

Sam swallowed a bit of her sandwich and offered her mom a meager smile. "I hope so."

20

Libby

Libby stood at the kitchen sink, absentmindedly washing the colander she'd used for spaghetti the night before. As she held it under the stream of water to rinse off any soap, she glanced up at the ceiling as if she could see through it to the bedroom she shared with Gabe. Was he really home? It almost seemed like a dream when he'd arrived at their house a little after midnight. He'd been so tired after the nine-hour drive that he'd barely had time to bring his small suitcase inside, kiss her goodnight, and fall into bed.

Footsteps sounded in the upstairs hallway, followed by the sound of a child tromping down the stairs.

"Where's Daddy?" Beth cried out as she bounded into the kitchen. Her eyes darted around the room, as though he might be hiding in a corner.

Libby smiled and held her index finger up to her mouth. "Shh." She pointed upward. "Daddy's still sleeping. He got home really late last night."

"Oh!" Beth's voice lowered to a stage whisper, but the

excitement on her face didn't diminish. "Is he going to get up soon?"

Libby shrugged. "I don't know. But we should let him sleep, okay? Maybe he'll be awake after you have breakfast."

"Okay." Beth didn't look convinced that this was the best plan, but she grabbed a bowl out of the cupboard and one of the many boxes of cereal from atop the fridge.

Libby opened the refrigerator and retrieved the milk, just in time to see Kaya plodding into the kitchen, clutching Little Bunny tightly in her right hand.

"Kaya," Libby asked in a low voice. "Do you want cereal too?"

Kaya nodded, and rubbed the sleep out of her eyes with one hand as she held up the stuffed animal. "She wants some too."

Libby sighed but grabbed a second bowl. If she didn't want to wake Gabe, it would be best to humor Kaya. Libby helped the girls get their cereal and milk, then did the same for Tommy when he came down a few minutes later. William rarely woke up before ten on the weekends unless he had to, so she put the milk away after serving the younger kids and joined them at the table with a fresh cup of coffee. After being woken up by Gabe's arrival last night, she'd had a hard time getting back to sleep, and now needed all the caffeine she could get.

She eyed the coffee. It was only her second cup, so she doubted it accounted for the nervous butterflies zooming around in her stomach. She'd barely seen Gabe last night and he'd been gone for close to six weeks. This was the longest they'd ever been apart since they were married, and she hadn't expected to feel so nervous about seeing him again. It was Gabe upstairs—*her* Gabe, not some stranger.

But, as much as she didn't want to admit it, things were different in their house. Although he was still her husband and her children's father, he was almost like a visitor in the household, with a suitcase full of his clothes and belongings he would take back with him. She'd been parenting their kids alone, with the exception of the video chats that Gabe had tried to do every few days, and she was already wondering whether it would be hard to go back to their new routines after Gabe left again.

"Daddy!" Beth shouted. She abruptly shoved her chair back, bumping the table. Libby barely had time to grab her coffee cup to keep it from being knocked over, and she wasn't quick enough to catch Kaya's cup of milk. Luckily, Kaya loved milk and had already drained at least three-fourths of the liquid, so not much spilled onto the table.

Libby pushed her chair back to grab the paper towels from the counter, but Gabe beat her to it.

"I've got it." He plucked a few sheets from the roll and mopped up the milk, then leaned forward to plant a kiss on Libby's lips.

Her heart raced and she barely had time to respond before he was whirling away to put the used paper towels in the compost bin and bending down to hug each of the kids in turn.

Gabe's presence energized the room, and the kids' voices rose as they urged him to take a seat next to Libby. He winked at her as Beth brought him cereal and a bowl, and Kaya struggled to carry the half-full gallon of milk to the table.

"Why, thank you." He grinned at the kids. "Such good service at this establishment."

Beth beamed. "We missed you, Daddy."

He leaned over and kissed her forehead. "I missed you

guys too." He winked at Libby again, re-invigorating the butterflies in her stomach. "A lot."

Her face warmed and she took a gulp of coffee before looking up again. "I thought we might go to the beach park today—maybe have a picnic there?"

"Sounds great, honey." He reached for her hand under the table, holding it as he finished his breakfast. He didn't release it until he stood from the table to clear away his dishes and hers. "At this rate, I think William's going to be having lunch instead of breakfast."

"I'll go wake him up!" Kaya said.

"Wait," Libby chided her. "Let him sleep a little longer. No one wants to deal with a grumpy William."

Tommy scrunched up his face. "Yeah, he's a real grouch these days. He never wants to play with us anymore."

Gabe shot Libby a questioning look.

She shrugged. "He's in that preteen stage."

"I'll have a talk with him while I'm home," Gabe said.

Libby nodded but didn't say anything. She hadn't told Gabe about William running away or about his recent change in behavior. Her husband had enough to worry about and didn't need to hear about the negative impacts of his absence on the kids.

A few hours later, they all piled into Libby's minivan and drove a few miles to what they affectionately called the "beach park." The city park was situated at the mouth of the Willomish River, where it flowed into Willa Bay. It was a family favorite, due to its elaborate playground, grassy fields overlooking the bay, and the easy access to the beach.

The younger kids dashed over to the playground as

soon as they arrived, while William helped his mom and dad carry the picnic supplies to a table near the play area.

Libby caught William looking wistfully at a father and son playing football out in the field. "Hey, William," she called out to him as he set a jug of water on the table.

"Yeah?"

"Look in that blue bag your dad left on the picnic bench."

He shot her a quizzical look but did as she'd asked. When he unzipped the bag and pulled out a few baseballs and a football, his face lit up. "Dad remembered!"

She grinned. "He's been looking forward to playing with you."

Gabe walked up to the table, pulling a heavy, green rolling ice chest filled with food behind him. "That's the last thing from the car!" He left it near the table and clapped his eldest son on the shoulder. "You up for tossing the football around a bit?" He glanced at Libby, as if asking if it was okay to leave her alone with the picnic preparations. She nodded and gave him a thumbs up, so he turned expectantly to William.

A huge smile stretched across William's face. "I'll race you." He jetted toward the middle of the field.

Gabe groaned, then took off after him in a slower jog.

Libby watched them play for a few minutes, then organized the table with the sandwiches, chips, veggies, and brownies she'd brought. They all looked like they were having a good time, so she sat on the picnic bench and looked out toward the bay at the other end of the park. The afternoon sun made the water glitter like it had been laced with diamonds but did little for the ambient temperature. She shivered and pulled her scarf tighter around her neck, tucking it into the neckline of her jacket. Why had she thought a picnic in the park in February was a good idea? From the warmth of her kitchen that morning, it had seemed like a fun outing, but now she was starting to regret it.

Laughter down at the playground caught her attention. Her girls were chasing Tommy around the play structure, and they were all laughing so hysterically that Libby couldn't help but smile. She turned her attention to Gabe and William. They were huddled together, with Gabe showing William how to do something with the football.

A few minutes later, she gave in to the cold and called everyone to come and eat. They jogged back to the table, bumbling around until she assigned each person a seat. Soon, they were all eating happily, trading stories about their week. She hugged her arms to her chest, but happiness warmed her heart. This was why they'd braved the cold. It was almost like Gabe had never left.

That evening, they went to dinner at her parents' house. Normally, they'd all have dinner together on Sunday night, but because Sunday would be Valentine's Day, they'd opted to have it on Saturday instead.

Debbie hugged Gabe as soon as they walked in. "I'm so glad you're here. Libby and the kids have missed you so much—and the rest of us have too. It doesn't seem the same without you here."

"It's good to see all of you." He gave his mother-in-law a bittersweet smile and returned her embrace. "I have to admit, I didn't think I'd miss the chaos of family dinner, but it's so quiet in my kitchen in Idaho that I can barely stand it."

Libby blinked back a tear as she watched Gabe greet the rest of her family. He must be so lonely there by himself. She'd been so focused on how busy her own life had become that she hadn't stopped to consider what his new life must be like. Now, she regretted the times she'd envied his quiet apartment.

When they were all gathered around the dinner table, talk turned to Debbie's upcoming fundraiser.

"Are you excited, Mom?" Meg asked. "Zoe told me the event is the talk of the town."

Debbie smiled and set down her fork. "I have to admit, I'm a little nervous. I never thought it would get this much attention. I mean, I'd hoped it would be popular, but it's much bigger than I'd expected." She frowned. "Zoe's promised me she'll come up with a replacement for the tents that were damaged, but I'm still a little worried."

"If Zoe said it's fine, I wouldn't worry." Libby leaned over to squeeze her mom's shoulder. "I'm sure she's got everything under control."

"I hope so." Debbie pressed her lips together tightly.

"Oh, you don't need to hope," Meg said mysteriously. "I happen to know there's a plan in the works."

Debbie narrowed her eyes at Meg. "What is it?"

"I can't tell you, but just don't worry about it." Meg and her boyfriend, Taylor, exchanged knowing glances.

Debbie eyed each of the adults in turn. "Does anyone know what Meg is talking about?"

"Nope." Libby fought a grin. It was nice to see her super-organized mom a little unsettled for a change.

Debbie looked over at her youngest daughter. "Sam, do you know?"

Sam's eyes were glazed over as if she'd been thinking of something else the whole time, and she shook her head for a moment before answering. "Know what?"

Debbie sighed. "I guess we'll all just have to wait until next weekend."

Libby winced slightly, but she didn't think anyone noticed besides Gabe, who squeezed her hand. Everyone was excited about the fundraiser, but Gabe was leaving on Monday morning and wouldn't be able to attend. She shot him a smile and forced herself to appear happy for her mom's sake. Luckily, she'd be managing the catering for the fundraiser, so she'd be able to throw herself into her work to avoid thinking about Gabe's absence.

Later that night, after she and Gabe got the kids to bed and he was in the shower, she checked her planner to make sure she hadn't forgotten to do anything. At the top of the day's to-do list, she'd written *CHECK OIL!* in big block letters. When Gabe lived at home, they'd divided the household chores, and car care had been his responsibility. Now that he wasn't there full-time, she'd had to assume the necessary task.

Her eyes flickered to the clock on the living room wall. She hated dealing with the messy oil. It was already nine o'clock. It could wait, right? Maybe she'd even be able to get Gabe to do it for her.

But no. He was still in the shower, and if she put it off until tomorrow, she might forget. With the way her aging minivan ran through oil, that could spell trouble. Reluctantly, she got up from the couch and went into the garage to grab a quart of motor oil. Sure enough, when she pulled the dipstick out, it was down a quart from when she'd checked it last month. She poured it into the well and screwed the cap back on tightly.

Just as she clicked the hood of the car into place, she heard the front door open and shut.

"I didn't expect to find you out here." Gabe walked toward her as she cleaned some stray oil off her hands with a baby wipe she'd brought with her for that purpose.

She shrugged. "My car needed some oil."

"I could have done that for you." Her husband

sounded almost insulted that she hadn't asked him—or was that a tinge of disappointment in his voice?

"It's okay. I need to get used to doing it myself. I did it last month too. It's not a big deal." She met his gaze in the dim light from the lantern-style fixture attached to the exterior of the garage.

"But I usually do it for you." He took the empty oil container from her and tossed it into the garbage can lined with a plastic bag that they kept outside for such occasions. "I feel bad that I've left you alone to deal with everything at home."

"It's just a quart of oil." She flashed him a bright smile, hoping to reassure him. It wasn't his fault that he'd had to move for his job, and taking care of her own car actually gave her a strange sense of accomplishment. "It wasn't like I had to overhaul the engine, or anything."

He sighed. "I know. It just feels like I'm not doing enough."

Libby grabbed Gabe's shoulders and made him face her. Peering into his eyes, she said, "I don't mind. This can't be easy for you either. The kids and I are doing fine here, but we're looking forward to joining you in Idaho."

In response, he kissed her, then pulled her close against him. She pressed her cheek to his chest, listening to the beating of his heart. They were out in the driveway where anyone could see them, but she was so glad to have him home that she didn't even care. She hadn't been entirely truthful about being excited to move to Idaho, but she *was* looking forward to once again having all of their family living in the same house.

21

Debbie

Debbie left her house a few hours before the Skamish County Cancer Society fundraiser was due to start. She wanted to get to the Inn at Willa Bay early to hammer out a few last-minute details with Zoe and Tia. Libby would come later with Debbie's husband, Peter, and the catering crew. Sam planned to attend the event as well.

"Good luck, honey." Peter caught Debbie on her way out and gave her a quick goodbye kiss. "Not that you need it. You've put so much effort into the fundraiser and I know it'll be amazing."

She forced a smile for him, but her stomach rolled as she plodded down the cement walkway to her sedan. She leaned over from the driver's seat to check the contents of her laptop bag for the third time in the last ten minutes. There were so many moving parts to an event of this magnitude, and she didn't want to forget any of her checklists at home.

She gripped the wheel tightly and forced herself to

relax by uttering a few reassurances out loud: "It's going to be great, Debbie. Nothing will go wrong. It's going to be great."

When she arrived at the Inn at Willa Bay, she parked her car in the guest parking lot, exited the vehicle, and slung the strap of her laptop case over her shoulder. Fortune had smiled upon her somehow, and it was shaping up to be a beautifully sunny—albeit chilly—day in the middle of February.

Seagulls soared overhead, seemingly unbothered by the cool weather. Debbie wasn't so fortunate. She shivered and zipped the front of her brick-red winter coat all the way up to her neck. She hoped it wouldn't be too cold for the guests. When she and Zoe had discussed having the event outside, Zoe had assured her the guests wouldn't be chilly at all with the high-capacity heaters they used in the event tents.

The Inn's grounds were in tip-top shape, and they'd even planted colorful flowers along the paths. Although Debbie wasn't sure they would survive the next frost, she was grateful for the cheeriness the flowers brought to the winter landscape. She raised her head to briefly soak in a few rays of sunlight, then frowned as she looked in the direction of the main lawn.

Where was everything? Nothing had been set up in the location they'd agreed on. Even if the tents she'd ordered had been destroyed in the snowstorm, Zoe had promised her she'd figure something out.

Debbie scanned the area, her gaze drifting over the white gazebo overlooking the bay and a few wood benches, but there weren't any tents in sight. Fear knotted in her stomach. Had Zoe decided to put them further back on the property for some reason? Maybe she'd had her crew set up closer to the cottages, away from the main lodge. From previous visits to the resort, she knew there was a small lawn area beyond the trees, but it wasn't what she had planned on. Debbie headed in that direction, grateful to be wearing her tennis shoes and street clothes instead of the nice dress and heels she would put on later.

When she reached the small stand of trees, her worst fears came true. There wasn't anything here either. There had to be some mistake. Zoe wasn't likely to mess up on the date, and neither was her assistant, Tia.

What was going on? Her mind raced with an excess of anxious thoughts.

Debbie hurried back across the grounds. There had to be a reasonable explanation. Over 200 guests were registered for the event and she wasn't about to let them down. She'd worked too hard and the cause was too great.

When she neared the guest house, she slowed her pace as a thought occurred to her. Was this part of Meg's surprise? She'd assumed her daughter meant that she had something to show her at the newly renovated cottage she shared with her co-worker, Tia, but had it actually been about the fundraiser?

Debbie climbed the stairs to the entrance and stepped into the warm lobby. Celia greeted her at the front desk with a wide smile. "I can't believe the big day has finally come."

Debbie shook her head. "Me neither." At times, she'd wondered if the day would ever arrive. It seemed like she'd been planning the fundraiser for years instead of a mere six months. She eyed the elderly woman, who was a long-time friend of Debbie's mother, Elizabeth Arnold. "Uh, do you happen to know where Zoe set up the tents? I didn't see them out front."

Celia's eyes sparkled, and she motioned to the hall behind the reception area. "I might know a little something about that. Let me get Zoe to explain though. She's working in the kitchen right now, checking on some last-minute details."

"Thanks." Debbie offered her a tight-lipped smile, but her curiosity was piqued. Everyone else seemed to be in on a big secret, and she was the last to know.

Celia moved out from behind the desk and limped toward the kitchen, her carved wooden cane tapping a steady beat with each step she took.

A few minutes later, Zoe emerged from the long hallway and leaned in for a quick hug. "I'm glad you're here. We have a lot to show you."

Now Debbie was more confused than ever. "I'm a little afraid to ask, but how did everything turn out with the tents? Did you decide to put them somewhere else?"

Earlier in the week, Zoe had left her a voicemail assuring her that everything was working out perfectly, but she hadn't left any details about potential changes to where they'd hold the event. Debbie may not have seen anything set up outside, but she also wasn't familiar with the Inn's entire grounds, so maybe there was a suitable grassy space elsewhere on the property.

A mischievous grin spread across Zoe's lips. "Oh, I think I'll let Meg tell you about that. She should be here soon."

So, her middle daughter *was* in on whatever was going on with the fundraiser. Debbie narrowed her eyes at Zoe, but the younger woman stayed mum and pretended to be engrossed by some paperwork at the front desk. Debbie opened her mouth to ask Zoe another question, but, as if on cue, the front door opened and Meg popped into the lobby.

"Oh good, you're here." Meg wrapped her arms around Debbie and squeezed her tightly.

"Honey." Debbie kept her voice as level as she could manage, although she was dying to find out what they had planned for her. "I hear you have a surprise for me."

Joyful laughter bubbled out of Meg, and she reached for Debbie's hand. Her daughter's enthusiasm boosted Debbie's spirits and increased her confidence that she and Zoe had the situation handled—but it didn't make Debbie any less nervous. "I thought you'd never ask. Come with me." She led Debbie out the back door at the end of the staff hallway and onto an oyster-shell path that snaked its way around the roots of tall evergreen trees, making its way to the far side of the property.

"Where are we going?" Debbie had never taken this route before and couldn't think of where her daughter was taking her.

"You're really not good at surprises, are you?" Meg teased. They continued down the path until they stood in front of a giant white barn with a gambrel-style roof.

So, this wasn't about the fundraiser after all. Debbie's heart sank as she eyed the massive building. "Honey, I really do want to see your new restaurant space, but I've got to get things ready for my event. Can we do this later?"

Meg gestured to the large structure in front of them. "Mom. This is the surprise." She threw open the wide doors, revealing a sunlit space.

Debbie sniffed the air and was rewarded with a fresh scent. The last time she'd seen the historic barn, there were still piles of junk in every corner and it had smelled as though it hadn't been long since it had stabled horses. Now, the stalls on one side had been renovated into private dining nooks that would be ideal for a romantic dinner date. They'd removed the stalls on the other side, creating a large open space for guests to gather. Every surface had been scoured and freshly whitewashed, the wood panels stained with a beautiful gray tint.

To her surprise, the main area of the barn had been set up with round tables, royal-blue linens, and crystal water glasses. Debbie's breath caught. It was lovely—more beautiful than she ever could have imagined.

"This is for the fundraiser?" she managed to get out.

Meg's head bobbed, and she peered anxiously at her mother. "Do you like it?"

"I love it." Debbie couldn't help gawking at the barn's transformation. Heat lamps stood in every corner, ensuring the space would be warm enough for all of the guests. Unlike the tents they'd planned to use, there now appeared to be plenty of room for guests to mingle with others who weren't seated at their same table. "But how did you get it all done in time? I thought you weren't going to work on it until the cottage renovations were complete."

Meg shrugged, but her face shone with pride as she surveyed her surroundings. "After we found out your tents were ruined, my co-owners and I agreed that getting the barn ready for your fundraiser took priority over everything else on the docket." She laughed and gestured behind her to the space under what had once been a hayloft. "Although, as you can see, we're not quite ready for me to open my restaurant yet."

Debbie followed Meg to the back of the barn, where they'd blocked the unfinished space from view with a wall of white wooden trellises. Like the rest of the building, the future kitchen space had been cleared, but not yet equipped with most kitchen appliances. A clean, but aged commercial refrigerator had been hooked up, along with a sink and prep table suitable for catering.

Meg rested her hand on the edge of the trellis. "I'm still working on the final design for my kitchen, but at least now I have a good idea of what everything will look like once it's finished."

Debbie's throat choked up. Her daughter had not only recognized beauty in the old, dilapidated barn when nobody else had, but also envisioned everything it could be. "I'm so proud of you for pursuing your dreams, and I can't wait to have my first meal in your very own restaurant."

Meg's cheeks flushed. "Thanks, Mom." She glanced at her watch. "But enough with the talk about my restaurant —we've got a fundraiser to host!"

Staff members had come into the barn and were busy with final preparations. After going through all the final details with Zoe, Debbie checked in with Libby, who'd just walked in with their catering team. Tia noticed the group's arrival and directed them to the rudimentary kitchen.

Debbie waved at Libby, who wore the professional-looking white blouse and black skirt she usually wore for catering jobs. Libby waved back and walked over to join Debbie, just on the other side of the makeshift trellis wall.

"This is Meg's surprise?" Libby's gaze roamed over the barn's interior. "I wasn't sure what to think when she said she had something for you, but this is better than I ever expected. People are going to flock to her restaurant when it opens."

"I know."

The sparkling white walls and floors had retained the charm of the historic barn, but now made a beautiful backdrop for an event venue. When Meg had first proposed using the barn for her future restaurant, Debbie hadn't been sure what to think. She should have known her daughter would be able to make it happen though. Libby might have been the one thought to possess the most forceful personality of her three daughters, but Meg and Sam had plenty of grit of their own.

"Do you need any help with getting things set up?" Debbie asked. Now that she'd turned any final preparations over to Zoe and Tia, she felt a bit adrift.

Libby shook her head. "Nope, I think we're fine. Zoe and Tia thought of everything we'd need."

"Well, if you need anything, just let me know."

Libby laughed. "Mom. This is *your* event. You've got enough to do here, and our staff is ready for this. You know this isn't my first catering job, right?"

Debbie hung her head. "I know. I just feel bad I'm not helping with that aspect of the event."

Libby put arm around Debbie's shoulders and gave her a light squeeze. "Don't even think about it. I've got everything under control. Besides, Gabe is gone so it's not like I have a date for this. I'm happy to be working to take my mind off of things."

A wave of sadness washed over Debbie, both for her daughter's situation and for the realization that she wouldn't have Libby there to help after the start of summer.

One of the catering staff waved at them, and Libby nodded back in acknowledgement. She turned back to her mother. "I'd better go, but I'll check in with you later.

Libby darted off toward the makeshift kitchen, and Debbie checked her watch. It was past time for her to get changed into her party clothes.

An hour later, Debbie stood to the side of the barn with her husband, surveying the event. Almost everyone that had purchased tickets had shown up. Guests milled around the large interior, and she heard many of them admiring the decor.

Out of the corner of her eye, Debbie spotted the

husband and children of her late friend, Diana, as they entered through the open barn doors. A twinge of grief mixed with a hint of guilt ran through her body. She and Diana had met while going through cancer treatments together, but while Debbie had made a full recovery, Diana hadn't been so fortunate. Debbie swallowed hard, excused herself from Peter, and made her way over to where Diana's family stood near the entrance.

"It's nice to see you again, Greg." She shook his hand and greeted the two preteen boys as well.

"Diana..." Greg's voice caught on his wife's name, and he cleared his throat before making another attempt. "She would have loved this."

The boys shifted awkwardly in what appeared to be new, black-leather dress shoes.

Tears welled in Debbie's eyes. "I wish she could have been here." She took a deep breath and smiled at him. "I think we're going to raise a lot of money for the Skamish County Cancer Society tonight though."

"I hope so. Diana would have appreciated you doing this in her memory." He looked at the photo of his wife that they'd placed on the sign-in table and blinked back tears. "Thank you for this." He seemed to notice that the boys were getting antsy. "I'd better find these two some-thing to eat before they get into trouble."

"There should be waiters going around with appetiz-ers." Debbie scanned the room for her catering staff's familiar white button-down shirts and black pants. She spotted one of the newer employees about twenty feet away and pointed at him. "I'd start with him. It looks like he has pigs in a blanket, so the kids should like it." In truth, the appetizers were actually garlic chicken sausages wrapped in puff pastry, but she figured the common name would be more appealing to young boys.

Diana's husband nodded. "Sounds right up their alley." He turned to the boys. "Alright boys, let's get some food. Maybe we'll even have some time to explore outside a bit before the dinner and auction start."

Debbie gave them a small wave as they walked away, then looked around to see if the rest of her family had arrived. Meg and Libby were both working the event, but she hadn't seen Sam yet, even though her youngest daughter had requested two tickets. Debbie recalled from their lunch at Wedding Belles a little over a week ago that Sam had been waffling about whether to go out on another date with someone she worked with. With any luck, she would bring him as her date tonight.

A little while later, she spotted Sam standing at a cocktail table in the far corner of the room, next to a man with brown hair and glasses. He was of average height and not as classically handsome as Sam's ex-boyfriend, Brant, but he wore a friendly smile as they chatted. Judging by the matching smile on her face, he made Sam happy too.

Debbie's husband, Peter, approached her and wrapped an arm around her waist. He pulled her close and whispered in her ear, "I'm so proud of you, honey."

Happiness filled her soul and she leaned into his embrace. With Libby soon leaving the state and her other daughters figuring out their own lives, she didn't know what the future would hold for any of them. For now, though, Debbie was going to simply enjoy the fruits of her hard labor and savor the success of the fundraiser.

22

Sam

"How many of these people do you know?" Andrew asked incredulously. "I grew up in a small town, but I guess we weren't as close as people are in Willa Bay."

Sam had to laugh. As soon as they'd walked into the barn for her mom's fundraiser, she'd been approached by a number of friends and acquaintances—all of whom wanted to know how she'd been doing since she moved the short distance away to Paddle Creek. "Oh, maybe only a few more—like those people." She gave him an impish smile and gestured to most of the crowd.

He raised an eyebrow. "Seriously?"

She laughed again. "Okay, okay. I don't know everyone here, but I grew up in Willa Bay and my family has been here for generations. I think my grandmother actually does know most of the guests."

She hadn't seen her grandmother yet, but Elizabeth Arnold would never miss an event like this, even if it wasn't hosted by her daughter. Sam scanned the room, pleased to see that all of the attendees looked like they were having a good time. Her mom had said it would be a big event, but Sam hadn't imagined there would be quite so many people. The high turnout would be beneficial for the auction later that evening though.

Good job, Mom, Sam thought. When Debbie found out last summer that her friend Diana had died, she'd been distraught. Hosting this event had been a huge commitment of both time and energy, but it had given her mom a way to honor her friend's memory. Sam continued scanning the crowd until she located her mom talking to someone near the podium at the far end of the barn.

Andrew followed her gaze. He lightly elbowed the side of her arm and pointed to the podium. "Is that your mother over there?"

She turned to him, cocking her head to the side. "Yeah. How did you know?"

He shrugged. "She has the same smile as you, and she looks like she's in charge."

"Really? Huh." Sam had never thought she looked like her mom and was surprised at how pleased she felt by his comment. "Maybe. Usually, people say my older sister, Libby, looks like our mom."

She looked around and quickly located Libby, busily instructing the catering staff on the other end of the room. She also caught a glimpse of Meg, and pointed both of them out to Andrew. "My dad should be here too, but I don't see him right now. I'll make sure to introduce you to everyone later." Out of the corner of her eye, she spotted Zoe making a beeline for them. She clutched Andrew's arm to alert him. "Incoming."

"Sam!" Zoe cried out. "I feel like it's been ages since I last saw you. How's everything going?" She eyed Andrew appraisingly. "Is this the famous Andrew?"

Sam's cheeks warmed. She'd known she'd have to introduce him to everyone tonight, and she'd been dreading it. All her life, she'd felt like she'd been under the microscope of her family and their close friends. It had been nice to get to know Andrew without having that added pressure.

Before Sam could respond, Andrew laughed nervously and stuck out his hand. "I don't know about famous, but yes—I'm Andrew Hodgins."

"I'm Zoe. Sam and I have known each other for close to a decade, and I'm so happy to meet you." She held out her hand, then withdrew it. "Oh, what the heck." She made a sound that was almost a squeal, and hugged Andrew before he knew what hit him. "I'm so glad to finally meet you."

After she released him, he took a step back and adjusted his glasses. "It's nice to meet you too."

Zoe shot him an apologetic look. "Sorry, I'm a hugger." She turned her attention to Sam. "Seriously, though, I'm glad the two of you were able to make it tonight. Your mom has done such an awesome job with this event." The phone in her hand buzzed loudly. She checked the screen and sighed. "Duty calls. But I want to talk to you more later, okay? Don't be a stranger around the Inn."

Sam nodded as Zoe scurried off toward the kitchen area.

"So, she's not even related to you?" Andrew asked. "How much enthusiasm should I prepare for from your actual family?" While his tone was joking, his expression was a little uncertain.

Sam patted his shoulder reassuringly. "Zoe's just a people person. That's why she's so good at her job as the event manager here. She always seems to know what people need, even before they ask. Don't worry, my family isn't terribly intimidating, they're just close."

Her stomach fluttered from nerves. At least she *hoped* the introductions with her family would go well. After she'd chatted with her mom about Andrew, she'd decided to pursue a relationship with him, and they'd been out on both lunch and dinner dates since. She really liked him, and she wanted her family to like him too. However, if for some strange reason they didn't take to him, she wasn't going to let that affect her decision to date him.

"Uh, I think there's a woman waving at you from a few tables away." The noise level had risen in the barn, and he had to speak directly into her ear. His breath tickled at the stray hairs that hadn't made it into her updo, and she shivered with delight.

She refocused her thoughts and looked around. Tansy and her husband sat two tables away from where she and Andrew stood against a wall.

"Oh." She half-heartedly waved and smiled, then turned away from Tansy and faced Andrew. She knew her former teacher wanted an answer about the ballet studio. *Everyone* seemed to have something to say about what she planned to do with her future.

"Oh?" Andrew cocked his head to the side. "Is she not a friend of yours?"

Sam sighed. "She is. That's Tansy, the owner of the studio where Kimmy and I take ballet lessons." She swallowed hard. "I've kind of been avoiding her because I didn't know what to say about her offer to sell me the ballet studio."

He studied her face. "And have you made a decision yet?"

Sam's eyes flickered to Tansy, who was still looking in their direction. "No."

Tansy's grandmother, Lucia, had been so brave about taking on the role of Headmistress at Bayside Prep during WWII. She'd known it was the right thing to do, and even though she was scared, she'd done it. But what did that mean for Sam? The idea of owning the ballet studio intrigued her, but she loved her current job at Bayside Prep too.

Sam took a deep breath and amended her answer. "Yes. I know what I want to do. Do you mind if I speak with her alone?"

"No problem." He pulled her close and touched his forehead to hers. "Take all the time you need."

His show of support bolstered her resolve and she moved away from him and strode toward her old friend, who stepped away from her table and met her halfway. Sam hugged Tansy, exclaiming, "I love your dress." The other woman wore a red, flamenco-style dress that skimmed her ballet-toned legs at mid-calf.

"I love yours too," Tansy murmured. "I'm used to seeing everyone in their day-to-day or gym clothes, so it's strange to see them all dressed up." She pulled back from Sam and peered at her. "How are you doing?"

Sam smiled. "I'm good." She realized that, for the first time in months, she truly felt good. Making decisions about her future had taken more out of her than she'd expected. "Actually, I wanted to talk to you about the studio."

Tansy's eyes lit up. "Oh good. I've been meaning to ask if you'd given any more consideration to buying it from me."

"I have." Sam paused, gathering her thoughts. "As much as I love it, I don't think it's the right choice for me."

Tansy's face fell. "Oh."

"But," Sam said. "What would you think about me

taking on a part-time managerial role there? If you had some help, maybe you could keep the studio for a while longer and still have time to travel."

Tansy bit her lip and cast a glance at her husband, who was patiently waiting for her at their table. "Hmm." A glimmer of a smile spread across her face. "You know, that might work." She sighed deeply. "I didn't really want to sell the studio, but it *is* a lot to handle on my own."

Sam grinned at her conspiratorially. "I figured you didn't want to leave it either. You always look so happy there."

"I do love it." Tansy hugged her again. "Thank you, Sam. You've given me a lot to think about. Let's touch base about this next week, okay?" She glanced at Andrew, who was leaning against the wall and appeared a little at-sea in a room full of strangers. "Is this the young man that I've been hearing about?"

This was small-town life. She'd never mentioned Andrew to Tansy before, but somehow the older woman had heard all about him.

Sam shook her head, then laughed. Motioning for Andrew to join them, she said, "Let me introduce the two of you."

After they'd chatted with Tansy and her husband for a few minutes, Sam noticed Debbie alone at a bar-height cocktail table in the corner. "I think my mom might finally have a few minutes to spare, and I still haven't introduced her to Andrew."

"Good luck, honey," Tansy said. "I'm rooting for you."

Sam grabbed Andrew's hand and they wound their way through the clusters of guests and over to Debbie. As they grew closer, Sam slowed. She wished things were more normal between her and her mother. While she'd known that she didn't see a future for herself with the catering company, her mom was under a lot of stress with Libby leaving, and Sam didn't want to disappoint her.

Andrew halted. "What's wrong?" He squeezed her hand. "We can do this another time if you're not ready to have me meet your parents."

She smiled and squeezed back. "It's not that. I'm ready for you to meet them." She eyed her mom, who, by now, had seen them too. "I don't want to let my mom down by not joining her at the catering company."

"I'm sure she'll understand." He jutted his chin in Debbie's direction. "Shall we then?

When they reached her mom, Debbie moved away from the table and held out her hand. "I'm Debbie."

"Andrew." He shook her outstretched hand. "It's nice to meet you. Sam speaks of you often."

"Good things, I hope?" Debbie grinned at Sam.

Sam's thoughts were swimming. Her mom's big event wasn't the time to tell her. Then again, Debbie seemed to be in a great mood. Maybe this *was* a good time.

"Alright, spit it out," Debbie ordered. "What aren't you telling me?"

Sam gaped at her mom. Had her deliberations been that obvious? "Um..." Andrew nudged her, and she blurted out, "I'm happy to help with the catering business when you're extra busy, but I can't do it full-time."

Debbie threw her head back and laughed. "Is that all? I'd already assumed you weren't interested."

"You did?"

Debbie shrugged. "You didn't seem that excited about it, and I've seen how your face lights up when you talk about your work at Bayside Prep. I only wanted to offer you the role in case you needed a backup plan."

"Oh." A wave of relief flooded over Sam. She'd

checked one more decision off her list and her mom hadn't even been the slightest bit upset. "Thanks, Mom."

Debbie grinned at Sam and threw her arms around her, whispering in her ear, "I just want you to be happy, sweetie."

Sam's eyes watered and she sniffed to hold back a tear. "I am."

"I'm so glad." Debbie released her and turned to Andrew. "Well, I'd better check on dinner preparations. Andrew, it was lovely to meet you, and I hope we'll see you at family dinner sometime soon."

"I'd like that." He shook her hand and then asked Sam, "Maybe we can check out the grounds a bit before dinner?"

"Sure."

"Have fun, you two." Debbie gave them a little wave and hurried off in the direction of the kitchen.

Sam and Andrew exited the barn and walked along the path toward the bay. The crisp air was both chilling and invigorating, and she found herself almost skipping along the path.

Andrew chuckled when they reached the overlook. "You seem to be in good spirits."

"I am." Sam beamed at him. "It's been such a rough year for me, and now it's like everything is coming together—the ballet school, my job at Bayside Prep, and, of course, you."

He smiled at her, and she gazed into his eyes. After a hesitant moment, their lips met softly. The kiss wasn't lengthy, but it was their first, and it was enough to send sparkles through her that rivaled the glittering lights of Whidbey Island across the bay.

"I've been wanting to do that for weeks," Andrew

admitted, still holding her close enough that she could feel his breath against her skin.

"Me too."

Sam lay her head against his shoulder, her face turned toward the bay. Being with Andrew made her happy, and, for the first time since the past summer, her life felt settled. Accepting the permanent position at Bayside Prep and dating Andrew didn't promise that life would always be easy, but she knew in her heart it was the right thing to do. A year ago, she would never have imagined all of the current blessings in her life—but she'd finally found her joy.

EPILOGUE

Jessa

Jessa pulled the cottage door shut behind her and carefully descended the porch steps to the walkway. Two weeks out from her surgery, she was still a tad wobbly at times, but every day was a little better than the one before. In fact, last night, she'd even escaped the resort grounds and ventured out to town for dinner with Celia. Today, she planned to take a leisurely stroll along the beach and then have lunch with Zoe and Meg at the Inn.

She'd quickly learned not to plan too much, because she never knew when the waves of exhaustion would hit. However, because of the Army, she was accustomed to staying busy, and now she didn't know what to do with so much free time. Once she received the all-clear from her military doctor, she'd be off convalescent leave. Then things would get real. She'd take three months of terminal leave first, and then she would be officially retired from the Army.

How had twenty years gone by so fast? She hadn't

even considered leaving active duty for at least another five years, so she'd put off any thoughts of retirement—until she'd been diagnosed with the brain tumor. Although her prognosis was good and she'd been assured she could return to active duty, the idea of major surgery had forced her to think more about being closer to family and readjusting her priorities. At the time, retirement had seemed like a good option, but now she needed to figure out what she was going to do with the rest of her life.

The thought was sobering. She picked her way down the stairs to the beach, holding on to the railing her brother had installed for easier and safer access. She'd avoided the gravelly sand until today, but she thought she was strong enough now to manage the uneven terrain.

It was wonderful to be back on the beach. She perched on a weather-beaten, water-scoured log to rest and survey her surroundings. The tide was out, and the beach stretched in both directions as far as she could see. Behind her was the historic guest house of the Inn and the beautiful gazebo Shawn had restored. Growing up in Tacoma, she'd never known the Inn existed, much less that her long-lost grandmother lived there. It still struck her as surreal to be a partial owner of the Inn at Willa Bay.

Was her future with the Inn? Or was it somewhere else entirely? Since the moment she'd enlisted in the Army, she'd been happy to go wherever they sent her. Now, though, she had so many options—and only a few months to figure it out.

She took a deep breath of the salt-scented air and let the beach work its magic on her. Things would work out. The doctor seemed convinced that she'd make a full recovery, and she would have an Army retirement to fall back on if she didn't find a job right away. It may not be enough to support a life in the Pacific Northwest, but she could always move somewhere with a lower cost of living.

A seagull flew overhead, crying out orders to a friend further down the coastline. Waves lapped at the shore and the sun peeked out from behind a cloud, warming her cheeks as she turned her face upward. *It's going to be okay, Jessa.*

"Are you talking to yourself?" A woman teased from the stairs leading up to the resort. "Someone said they saw you head down here, and I thought I'd grab you for lunch."

Jessa whirled around. She laughed when she saw Meg standing there. "I didn't think I was talking out loud, but I guess I was."

Meg chuckled too. "I do it all the time, especially down here on the beach. There's something about it that makes you feel comfortable with your thoughts."

"I don't know if I'd say I was comfortable with them, but my brain is definitely in overdrive." Jessa pushed herself away from the log and stretched her legs to work out any cricks.

"Do you want to talk about it?" Meg stepped onto the sand and walked in Jessa's direction, stopping a few feet away from her.

Jessa stared at the kelp beds revealed by the low tide. She wasn't sure if it was her imagination, but she thought she'd seen a tiny crab scurrying across a piece of drying seaweed. She'd always loved searching the tidepools for sea life when she was a kid, and it was good to be back near the water. Next to her, Meg cleared her throat, bringing Jessa into the present.

"Sorry." Jessa sighed and returned her attention to Meg. "I don't know if I want to talk about it or not."

Meg nodded, but didn't say anything.

Jessa uttered a self-deprecating laugh and threw her hands in the air. "I don't think I really know much of anything right now."

"It must be difficult to have your life turned upside-down," Meg observed. "Are you thinking about staying around here for a while? I'm sure Celia and Shawn would love for you to stay in the area." She quickly added, "And the rest of us would too, of course."

"I don't know." Jessa traced her shoe across the sand, forming a straight line that would make her physical therapist proud. "I don't want to be a bother."

Meg cocked her head to the side. "You know you own part of the Inn, right? You have every bit as much of a right to be here as the rest of us do."

Jessa sighed. "I know, but the rest of you are actively involved with running the resort. I can't just sit in my cottage doing nothing."

Meg eyed her thoughtfully. "What would you think about partnering with me on the restaurant? Shawn said you have experience with managing catering events, so you'd be a natural for the business side of it. Goodness knows I'd rather be in the kitchen than managing staff and the day-to-day operations."

Help with the restaurant? Jessa had toured the barn, but other than that, she hadn't heard much about Meg's upcoming venture. "What would that entail?"

Meg laughed. "I don't know, I hadn't even thought about it until just now, but you really would be helping me. Starting my own restaurant has been much more work than I anticipated."

"I don't know." Jessa stifled a yawn. Even the short walk to the beach had taken a lot out of her. "I'm still recovering from my surgery, so I wouldn't be much help for a while."

"I'll take any assistance I can get." Meg beamed at Jessa and gestured up at the barn, barely visible from where they stood. "We can talk more about it as you start feeling better, okay?"

Jessa studied Meg for a moment. The other woman looked hopeful, which buoyed Jessa's own spirits. Maybe there actually was something to the partnership she'd proposed. This could be good for both of them. "Okay." A smile spread across Jessa's face as she imagined herself in the finished restaurant. "I think I'd like that."

AUTHOR'S NOTE

Thank you for reading The Riverside Dance Studio! If you're able to, please consider leaving a review for it.

If you haven't read Willa Bay's sister series, the Candle Beach Novels, check out Book 1, Sweet Beginnings.

Happy reading!

Nicole

ACKNOWLEDGMENTS

Thank you to everyone who's helped me with this book, including:

Editor: Devon Steele

Cover Design: Elizabeth Mackey Design

Made in the USA
Las Vegas, NV
21 August 2024

94204878R00135